S0-BEZ-117

Dance With Me

Winifred Madison

SCHOLASTIC BOOK SERVICES
New York Toronto London Auckland Sydney Tokyo

Cover Photo by Owen Brown

ISBN 0-590-31769-5

12 11 10 9 8 7 6 5 4   3 4 5 6/8
                Printed in the U.S.A.   06

Dance With Me

A Wildfire Book

WILDFIRE TITLES

1.

On the night of the Spring Prom, Jennifer Cowles, dressed in a silky pink evening gown of her own making and pale pink evening sandals, was sitting before the television in the Cowles' living room. This in itself was surprising. That she was withdrawn, and silent, and barely saw what went on in the flickering movie was even more unusual.

It would be difficult to imagine a more romantic evening for the dance. The last pinks and oranges of a sunset in late April had already given way to the deep blue of a night whose mild air promised summer. The waxing moon spread a luminous glow over the gently rolling landscape of the northern California Central Valley. The Cowles' ranch, a white, four-square Victorian house that rose primly from its setting of garden and orchards, was bathed tranquilly in the silvery night.

The house rang with sounds that suggested everyone was high-spirited and all was well. Giggles escaped from the kitchen where Mrs. Cowles joked genially with two small 4-H girls who had come over to make ginger-

1

bread. Mr. Cowles and Kenneth, Jennifer's older brother, hammered and banged away at the addition they were making to the living room. Bruce, Jennifer's younger brother, stretched on the floor, completely absorbed in the spring catalogue of farm equipment. Terry, Jennifer's twelve-year-old sister, already decked out in white shorts though it was only April and not really warm enough, chewed gum as she practiced baton twirling, keeping her eye on the television screen at the same time.

Only Jennifer was out of phase. She had looked forward to the Prom for months, had bought expensive material and spent hours sewing, ripping, and resewing the Vogue Paris-designed dress for this, her first formal dance. Unaccustomed to makeup, she had experimented with a touch of eye shadow and a light lipstick. Would Russ notice?

"Jennie, you've never looked prettier!" her mother had exclaimed.

"Looks as if our daughter's growing up!" Mr. Cowles had said, glancing up from his *Farm Journal.* He showed his pride, but a touch of sadness betrayed him, as if she were growing up all too quickly.

And then the phone had rung. "Jennifer? I'm afraid I'll be a little late. Bonnie Lass is going to calve tonight. She *would!* Still it shouldn't take too long. I'll get there as soon as I can, okay?"

Now, two hours later, Jennifer slumped in her chair in front of the screen.

"Hey, if Russ doesn't get here soon, you're gonna miss the whole Prom," Terry said.

"I know it," Jennifer snapped, immediately aware that her voice showed all too clearly her mounting irritation. Still, she defended Russ. "He's not staying away because he wants to. He can't help it if the most valuable cow in the herd decides to calve tonight."

"Well, I wouldn't stand for it," Terry said. "After all, who comes first, a girl or a cow? Why can't Mr. Steele take care of Bonnie Lass?"

"Because Russ is stubborn, I mean independent, and he wants to do it himself. Bonnie is his most valuable cow and it's possible he could lose both her and her calf. Anyway, the Steeles are away at some kind of political dinner and the vet's out of town this weekend."

"If it were me," Terry continued, "I'd go to the Prom by myself."

Jennifer would have thrown a pillow at her sister, but the kitchen telephone rang and she jumped up to answer it.

"Jen? It's me again. Listen, I'm awfully sorry, but Bonnie Lass is having a rough time of it. I'll come as soon as I can."

She slumped in her chair and gazed absently at a shampoo commercial in which a beautiful girl with hair as long, blonde, and fair as Jennifer's, turned slowly toward the camera and then looked up so that her profile merged with that of a man who was impossibly handsome. "My love shampoo," the girl whispered, and Jennifer thought that idiotic.

And yet she said the word to herself. Love. She was ready for it now; she thought about it a great deal, when she should have been thinking of other things.

Did Russell really love her? She couldn't tell. He was handsome, intelligent, strong, and he could compete successfully with any screen hero. Yet, there he was at home with his cow and here she was waiting.

Of course, he can't help it and I wouldn't have it any other way, she argued with herself fiercely. And yet, it wasn't the first time she'd been let down. There was the time the 4-H Club was going to go to a roller skating rink in Sacramento. A water main had broken on the Steele Ranch and he had stayed home to help fix it. When the Steeles and Cowles were going to see Terry in her first leading role in a play at the Junior High, one of the Steele's ranch hands had become ill and because the plowing had to be done, Russ had phoned his apologies and spent more than half the night plowing.

That was ranch life and she may as well accept it. But to miss the Spring Prom? It was too cruel. The ranch would go on and on, but there were few proms left for either Russ or herself. They were juniors now; there would be one more year of school and that would be the end of it.

"Anyone for hot gingerbread? Milk? Coffee?" Mrs. Cowles called out as she came

4

from the kitchen and set down on the oval oak dining room table a tray of steaming gingerbread and a bowl of whipped cream.

"Me!" Bruce cried, springing up and sampling the whipped cream with a none-too-clean finger before his mother could stop him. Terry put down her baton and said she would have only a tiny slice because she had to watch her figure.

"Jennie? C'mon, dear, you may as well enjoy this. Sara and Betsy are fantastic gingerbread makers."

The little girls giggled and Mr. Cowles asked for a piece at least four by four inches since he wasn't on a diet like Terry and if only Jennifer would join them. . . .

"No thanks," she said, tossing one foot over the arm of her chair, as if she'd forgotten she wasn't wearing jeans and boots. He's not coming, he won't make it, it's getting too late, was all she could think as she bit her thumb. Then, unexpectedly she was caught up in a television drama.

A party of six laughing young people were piling into a sports car. The camera darted from one smiling face to another. The car, photographed from varying distances, drove along a curving road with occasional glimpses of the California coast, then parked at a public beach. Everyone tumbled out, wind blowing their hair, sun sparkling on them as they carried picnic baskets, towels, and blankets to the beach. Two blonde persons were glimpsed putting on black diving suits. A couple lay on the beach lazily sunning themselves. The camera focused on the third couple as they walked along the beach, sea-gulls screeching overhead and a ship on the far horizon.

If only I were one of them . . . The thought arose spontaneously, alarming her, for in the past few months she had found herself wishing to be somewhere else other than in this peaceful, agricultural valley, longing to escape to another place, to become part of a different kind of life. Television proved that choices could be made and other lives could be lived. Yet, this desire seemed to her a shameful, treacherous thing, disloyal to everyone around her. It was too puzzling. She had always been so satisfied with her life on the ranch. So why seek something elsewhere?

Now the camera closely followed the couple who had gone walking along the water's edge. They had come to a long stretch of rocks and they scrambled over them, stopped to watch a tide pool, and then continued, jumping from one rock to another with remarkable nimbleness until at last, breathless, they sat on a flat rock high above the crashing surf. The young man's profile filled the screen, then the girl's softly de-lineated features as she listened to him.

"Chris, we have to talk. I think you know that. Don't you?"

Her eyes rose to meet his, then fell.

"Chris, there's so much I want to say. How beautiful you are! How I haven't been able to sleep since I've met you. Really, that's the

6

truth. There can never be anyone else for me ever. Only you."

Their faces merged into a long, breathtaking kiss, which faded when a commercial for Kentucky Fried Chicken came on. Now a set of tanned, vibrant, glamorous young adults were sitting around a swimming pool. Jennifer turned down the volume of their laughter and listened to the voices from the dining room. Her father who only at dinner time had gone on and on, complaining of taxes, was now pulling out his repertoire of riddles, while the little girls howled and Bruce, that natural comedian, added to the glee. Jennifer would have liked joining them, but the T.V. drama continued.

This time it showed the hero and heroine walking back from the rocks, shuffling their feet through the wavelets and holding hands, glowing with happiness as though they had all the time in the world. Time to fall in love, that was it.

"If only I could be there, just once . . ." she dreamed. The next minute she stood up and turned off the television with such decision that her mother glanced at her from the other room.

What's the matter with me? There's Russ, having a dreadful time and here I am acting like a perfect idiot! she thought.

This was not the first time she had received what she believed was an ESP message from Russ. This time it was SOS. He needed her.

She ran up the Victorian staircase to her room, a farmhouse room with white curtains over the dormer windows, wallpaper of old-fashioned daisies, and a quilt, made by her grandmother, on the white metal bed. An oversized photograph of Russ hung on the wall, and above her desk were flanked an assortment of gold, white, and blue ribbons she had won at various competitions.

Two kittens on her bed watched with wide blue eyes as she slipped out of the dress, which she had spent so many hours of painstaking work and left it lying on the floor. She kicked off her dancing shoes, but carefully peeled off her panty hose and put them away in a drawer where the kittens could not claw them. She pulled the pins that held her hair up in its triumphal crown and shook it so that it tumbled down over her shoulders and back. Now she put on jeans, socks, boots, an old navy blue sweatshirt, and a kerchief for her hair, the whole transformation taking less then two minutes.

She stopped in the dining room to explain.

"Oh Jen, you're not giving up on the dance?" Her mother was disappointed.

"It doesn't matter. It's more than half over. I'm going to help Russell."

Mr. Cowles said nothing, but studied his daughter through his metal-framed glasses. She had been so lovely in that pink dress, but he liked the way she had decided to help Russ. "Jennie, you're a peach."

"I'll be back later," Jennifer called out and her voice sounded more normal now, direct and good-natured. She closed the front door behind her and went out into the starry night.

2.

Jennifer had seldom bicycled as fast as she did that night over the mile of narrow country road that separated the Steele ranch from the Cowles'.

Though they were neighbors, each ranch presented a different image of country life. The Steele ranch, with its spreading one-story house of whitewashed brick, had once been featured in the Sunday Supplement of the *Sacramento Bee*, and a new barn Mr. Steele had had built was once used as a model for the modern California farm. Every building, every field, every foot of acreage on this extensive ranch was kept in prime condition, for Mr. Steele would have it no other way. In comparison, the Cowles house, a white Victorian, though more charming than the Steeles' would ever be, was continually in need of repair. The barns and sheds could not hide the many patches they had received over the years, yet it had never occurred to Jennifer or any of the Cowleses to feel jealous about the Steeles' relatively secure position, their swimming pool, and Mrs. Steele's horses.

Jennifer bicycled up between the gray stone pillars that stood at the entrance of the Steele ranch and pedaled the quarter mile to the barn where Bonnie Lass would be waiting for her calf to be born. She immediately went to the stall where the young Guernsey lay, panting. Jen knelt beside her and stroked her. "Hang in there, Bonnie. You'll have your calf soon."

Any self-pity she had felt while waiting for Russ that night had vanished instantly as she looked into the suffering, dark eyes of this handsome animal, the prize of the herd. Jennifer had often witnessed and assisted in the birth of lambs and calves and knew what needed to be done. She had long marveled at the ease with which animals bear their young most of the time, but she knew all too well that birth did not always go smoothly. Sometimes a newly born calf or lamb could die and its mother might breathe her last as well.

Too weak to stand, Bonnie lay on her side breathing heavily, while Russ lay on the floor of the shed as he tried to check the positioning of the calf. His shirt and pants were wet with perspiration, although the evening air was turning brisk.

"I'm glad you came, Jen. I could use some help. The calf's in breach and I've been spending the last hour trying to turn it around. It's almost ready now. Hey, Bonnie, old girl, it won't be much longer!"

"Shall we use the rope, Russ?"

"Think we'd better. It feels like a good-sized calf. There, we're coming now!"

The cow grunted heavily and presently two hoofs appeared. Jennifer tied the rope around them expertly as Russ checked the head position as well as he could. It took all of his efforts and Jennifer's to help the struggling cow, but at last the calf was born. Russ, smiling with relief, pierced the sac that surrounded the newly born calf, who lay wet and quiet, looking around the scene with surprise as if to say, so this is what it's like out here. Jennifer found a clean piece of burlap sacking and dried off the wet calf, while Bonnie Lass struggled to stand, turning her head toward her firstborn. Then, although she had appeared on the verge of dying only a few minutes before, she now bent over and licked her son with her rough, wet tongue.

Russ and Jennifer watched, each of them silent, as if a miracle had taken place.

"It's always so wonderful when it happens. No matter how many times you've seen it, each newborn animal is brand-new and somehow so wonderful. You just want to applaud it or give thanks or something," Russ said awkwardly. He seldom expressed his sentiments, but Jennifer understood that he was moved and she put her hand in his.

"I feel that way, too, Russ. I love the way the mothers know just what to do."

Russ nodded. They watched the young calf as it struggled to stand on shaky legs and searched for his mother's teats.

"How do they do it, knowing exactly where to go? New animals always do."

When the calf had satisfied himself and

11

settled down to lie beside his mother, Russ knelt down to examine him, while Jennifer brought a pail of water so that Bonnie Lass could drink.

"Good girl, Bonnie Lass. You've sure got yourself a fine calf. Just think, someday this little fellow will be a big, hulking bull."

"He'll be valuable, too, Russ. I know you were a little worried when you paid so much for the breeding, but it's really worth it. You'll have a fantastic herd."

"Hope so. Thanks, Jen," he answered. His eyes were not on her, but on the newborn creature, who seemed ready to sleep after his long, difficult passage into the world.

"I wish I'd brought my camera," Jen said. She would have liked catching the whole scene: Bonnie Lass in labor, Russ helping, the new calf struggling to stand, and now Russ as he beamed proudly at the new calf. Never mind that the chambray workshirt was drenched and his jeans badly stained. At that moment Jennifer thought him magnificent, with a quality that all the handsome television heroes lacked.

He had eyes only for Bonnie Lass and the new calf. Later, he would put his arm around her shoulder and let her know he was grateful for her help. Once at a 4-H Club meeting he had said that girls could be as strong as boys. Take Jennifer, he had said, while she sat there tense, wondering what would come next: She was not only as strong as most boys, but she knew what she was doing. "As good as any boy," he had once said. Good old Jen! Was that how he thought of her?

Suddenly, that wasn't enough.

He was still beaming over the new calf. Then he turned to Jen to say something about him, and snapped his fingers, as if suddenly remembering.

"The Prom! I almost forgot. I'll wash up and be ready in two shakes."

"Russell." Her voice chilled. "See what time it is!" She held out her watch. "It's way after eleven. The dance is nearly over."

"Let's go anyway. I can be ready in a jif."

"It's nineteen miles to Freeville. If we're lucky we'd get there in time for the end of the last dance. No, thanks."

He scratched his head. "Jen, I'm really sorry. I guess Bonnie Lass didn't realize how much it meant to you to go to the Prom or she would have waited."

"It's all right, Russ. Don't say any more. It's perfectly okay. I understand." Jennifer spoke with such force that Russ lowered his gaze. It wasn't at all like Jen to burst out like this, for though the words in themselves were all right, the emotion behind them was troubled.

"You were sure helpful, Jennifer. I appreciate it, I really do. I'd have had a devil of a time if you hadn't come along. I could've lost . . ." He could not bear to finish the sentence; the thought of losing Bonnie Lass and the calf was too disastrous to contemplate.

"You'd have managed," she said calmly, believing that he could not fail at anything. He was made for victories, for nothing but success, and she would have told him so if she'd been able to find the words, but a car drove up toward the back of the house. In a few minutes Russ' mother walked up to them.

"Hello, hello! What are you two doing here? Isn't the Prom tonight? Hey, wait . . . good heavens, you're not quarreling.

"Of course not," Jennifer said.

"Bonnie Lass had her calf, a bull calf."

"She was early then? Russ, may I see?"

Although Mrs. Steele was dressed in a long, white, tailored evening dress, she had to see the new calf. She stepped carefully into the stall.

"Why, he's a beauty! Absolutely perfect! Mama Bonnie, aren't you proud of yourself, giving us all such a surprise!"

She had to hear all the details of the birth from Russ. "And then Jennie came over, thank heavens. She has the magic touch."

"Magic touch! Russ, *you* did all the hard work. I don't think a vet could have done better," Jennifer said, overwhelmed at his lavish compliment, for he was not given to praising others.

"He's right, though," Mrs. Steele said. "You're a marvel around animals, Jen. That's why I let you ride my horses."

"Thank you," Jennifer mumbled, because Mrs. Steele, like her son, did not throw compliments around loosely. It was clear that she had passed on her good looks to Russ.

14

Tall, slender, and wiry, she moved gracefully with the slightest suggestion of a swagger in her stride. Jennifer found a certain coolness in the gray eyes, but perhaps it was only her tremendous efficiency and capacity for work that gave that impression. Mrs. Steele was more than kind to Jennifer, although Russ' mother lacked that fuller, softer, and somehow "homier" warmth that drew everyone toward Jennifer's mother.

As they walked toward the house, Mrs. Steele asked, "Are you sure you can't make it to the Prom? It's not over yet. I'd even let you take the Alfa Romeo; you'd get there in five minutes."

"How about it, Jen?" Russ asked. It was somehow noble of him, for Jennifer suspected he really did not care about going and would do so only for her sake, which spoiled it for her.

"I'm afraid it's all settled. We're not going, but thanks for the offer of the car."

"If that's how it is, that's how it is. But it does seem a shame to miss it. Oh, well, there'll be other dances. We ought to celebrate the new calf. How about some champagne?"

Jennifer hesitated. She did not mind what others did, but she had decided that aside from an occasional glass of wine, drinking was not her style. Fortunately, Russ agreed with her. Mrs. Steele, sensing something was not quite right, suggested they raid the fridge.

"The two of you could go for a moonlight ride, but Lady Ranleigh's broken ankle needs another day of rest before we let her out. Maybe tomorrow. Russ, dear, you could do with some washing up."

Jennifer would have gladly gone riding, galloping over the fields on a night like this. More than once she and Russ had taken the horses for long rides; at such times the harmony between them was perfect. And Mrs. Steele appreciated their exercising the horses because it gave her some relief, for she worked hard and continually. She may have had the reputation of being a rich woman for whom the raising of horses was "a hobby," but she told Jennifer it was her vocation and she fully expected that in time, with proper care and breeding, the horses would more than pay for themselves.

Mrs. Steele excused herself, and Russ said he'd be right with her after he showered, so Jennifer found herself waiting in the kitchen. They are always working, she thought about the Steeles. Even when they go to a political rally or dinner, it has the feeling of something purposeful about it. Do they never have a good time just for the fun of it? Would my life be like that if Russ and I . . . ? She didn't finish the thought.

"How about something to eat?" Russ said, appearing in clean jeans and a sweater his mother had made for him. Unexpectedly Jennifer found him at that moment startlingly beautiful, as if seeing him for the first time, although she had seen him every day for most of her life. What was it about him, the clean, scrubbed look, the depth of

16

his eyes, which could be gray or blue, a certain grace as he moved?

"I'm not hungry, but you go ahead. Want me to make something for you?" If she had been embarrassed at the anger in her voice earlier that night, now she feared a certain tenderness had become too obvious. But perhaps Russ did not notice, for he sliced a long hard roll in two, smeared it with mayonnaise and mustard, and layered it generously with slices of roast beef, tomatoes, lettuce, and sliced pickles. Four black olives were at the side of his plate, and a tall glass of milk.

"Let me get one for you, too, Jen. You're going to have to help me eat this Mammoth sandwich. That's the name of it, you know. I created the Mammoth. But Super Mammoth is even better, with bananas and peanut butter."

She laughed, even tasted a corner of his Mammoth. He was still in raptures over Bonnie Lass and the new calf. She recognized that, having felt the same way each time her lambs gave birth.

"I think I'd better go home, Russ. You don't have to go with me. I've got my bike."

He put down his sandwich. "Are you all right? What's all this about 'I don't have to go with you.'"

"It's up to you. I didn't want you to feel that you had to."

"I'll go with you, Jennifer," he said quietly again.

They walked their bicycles across a stubbly field, took a dirt road that led to a distant pasture, left their bicycles, and walked up a hill on which an almond orchard had once been planted, but had been allowed to go wild at least for a year or two. Russ and Jennifer referred to this place as "top o' the world," even though the hill was hardly qualified for so grand a title. Still, this is where they went when they wanted to be alone. Russ lay on his back and looked up at the stars, while Jennifer sat beside him.

"What a night, eh, Jen? Wonder if there's a lucky star out there somewhere! I'd like to think that the new calf will be really special. So glad it's a male, since there's been four heifers in the herd so far this year."

"Good luck, that's what it is, no doubt about it," Jennifer said, though her voice sounded flat to her. Russ was doing well, but would he go on talking like this all night?

"You're not doing so bad, Jen. A herd of fifteen. Too bad about the one you lost with her lamb, but you've got a great start. I still think we ought to go up to Williams so you can see that breeder I told you about. You might be interested in a lamb or two from his herd. Want to drive over sometime?"

"Sure."

As a rule Russ kept quiet and then Jennifer would keep up the heavy end of the conversation, but on those occasions when he became expansive, "he breaks into a gallop that can't be stopped," his father had said about him. On this romantic night in the fresh, velvety air, would he go on and on,

18

talking of Jen's prospects and his, of their next moves, of the 4-H clubs in which they played such prominent roles, of the special animal husbandry course for which they each had won scholarships?

A scene from the television drama she had seen earlier flashed through her mind: the hero and his girl perched on the rocks above the surf, the warmth and tenderness in his voice as he told her that he loved her. Russ had never done this. Never.

But he didn't go on chattering after all, only lay quietly as the wind rustled through the leaves of the ancient trees. In the distance, the startled cry of a night creature was followed by a peaceful silence, broken intermittently by the hum of cars or trucks on the highway. A plane flew overhead, flashing its lights before disappearing.

At last Russ sat up and put his arm around her. He had done this often enough before and she had always been excited at his touch, but now she wondered if this was the arm of a man who loved her or only that of a good pal.

"You're quiet tonight, Jen. Usually you're worse than a magpie, chattering, chattering, chattering." He opened and closed his fingers and thumbs to suggest endless gabbing and she poked him, all in good nature. They became serious again.

"It's not that I talk so much, but that you're usually much quieter. Anyway, I don't have anything to say tonight."

"You're still feeling bad about the Prom, aren't you? I'm really sorry about it, Jen. I'd have liked seeing you in that dress, the one with that high fashion pattern, wasn't it?" He was trying hard to be kind.

She thought of the dress now lying on the floor of her room like something abandoned, — a rare occurrence — for she was fastidious about hanging up her clothes. She remembered the day she and her mother had gone shopping for the material in Sacramento and her mother had sharply drawn in her breath at the price of the material, but it was Jennifer's money that paid for it. She had felt the thrill of anticipation as the material was cut. This would be her first truly formal dance.

"Jennifer, there'll be other proms, other dances."

"Please don't keep saying that."

"I don't know what to say. I'm sorry, I'm sorry, I'm really sorry."

"Well, that's just too bad. I don't care about the Prom, anyway."

"Then, what do you want?" Russ asked, his voice low and hesitant.

"I don't know!" she cried, fearful of the threat of tears in her voice. Perhaps, if he held her and spoke his mind as the hero did in the drama, if he told her that he really loved her, that would be enough. Then again, maybe it wouldn't. She wanted something, but could not tell exactly what. She saw herself piling into a car with others, riding along the coast, running along a beach.

Russ, upset by the storm he sensed in the usually calm Jennifer, picked a long piece of grass, sucked on it, threw it away. Perhaps he was afraid to become more familiar now.

"I'd better go home. It's getting late," she said, standing up.

They walked silently through the orchard, picked up their bicycles, and pedaled back to the Cowles' ranch, now dark except for the light that Mrs. Cowles had left burning in the hall for Jennifer.

She put her bicycle away, letting it lean against the side of the house. Russ put his arms around her and pulled her toward him.

"Jen, you don't need evening gowns. You're pretty just as you are, in your jeans and that sweatshirt. I like the way it says I DRINK MILK on the back of it." He smiled, a gentle taunt, for she detested the smug words.

"This disgusting shirt! It was the first thing I grabbed. It's so dreadful."

"No, it's beautiful because you're wearing it. It's hard to put into words . . . you know, those things I'd like to say."

He pulled her close to him and his lips came down on hers. Then everything became right again as his arms held her close and she clasped hers around him, feeling the steely slenderness of his back. He did love her then, so much that they clung together too closely and he broke away suddenly.

"I'd better go, Jennifer," he said softly.

"Thanks for walking me home. And, Russ . . . good luck on the new calf. When will you name him?"

"When I think up the right name. Maybe you can help. Want to go riding tomorrow for a while?"

"Maybe. I'll think about it."

"Don't forget, we've got an important 4-H meeting tomorrow night to decide on summer plans. I'll call for you."

He was so sure of her. Too sure. "Maybe I'll go."

The coolness in her voice upset him. "Jen, what's bugging you? I don't understand.

"I don't know what to say to you, Jen. Maybe tomorrow . . ."

He didn't finish the sentence, but in her mind she finished it for him. By tomorrow, with luck, this balky animal, Jennifer, would see the light and become her old, sweet, compliant self once more.

"Russ, I've got to go. I'll call you. Okay?"

He held her close once more, kissed her fiercely before releasing her. He waited until she opened the tall doors that led to the living room. Frowning slightly, wondering what had gone wrong and then deciding not to worry about it anymore, he jumped on his tenspeed and raced home.

3.

That night Jennifer dreamed of a long, smooth beach beside an ocean that sparkled now green, now blue. She was running and Russ was chasing her, but as happens in dreams, neither of them seemed to move an inch. A ray of morning sun penetrated the white curtains of her bedroom and with that, she woke up. Twelve minutes after six. Late! She sprang out of bed and immediately saw the pink dress lying on the floor where she had left it.

Poor dress! How could she have treated it so badly. She picked it up, smoothed it, hung it carefully on a hanger, and covered it with a plastic garment bag to protect it. The uncertain moodiness of the previous night had vanished. She would wear the dress somewhere else. It would not be as exciting as if she'd worn it to the Prom, but still it would be new. There! She put it away in the closet.

Yesterday was strange, an off-day. Today would be fine, like most days. She dressed quickly and dashed outside to the pasture near the house where her sheep stayed. As they saw her come they ran to the fence, jostling each other as they sought her favors, baaing and maaing, all wanting to be touched and loved.

"You guys, you're like a bunch of little kids!" Jennifer said with pride and affection, as though they really were her children.

With help from Terry and Bruce, she had named them after television and movie stars. Now, Paul Newman and Robert Redford, sturdy Suffolk rams, were demanding to be recognized, pushing the ewes out of the way. But one of the more aggressive ewes, Bo Derek, worked her way to the forefront. The twins, Mork and Mindy, looked at her wistfully from the edge of the gathering. Someday soon, Jennifer was planning, she would spend a whole afternoon photographing them. She was careful to take the usual formal studies, the stiff expository kind of picture that was used to record each animal, but now she wanted more informal pictures, the black-faced Suffolks crowding, later the peacefulness as they lay sunning themselves in the pasture, or the young lambs gamboling lightly together.

She petted them, talking gently, addressing each one by name. She saw each of them as personalities; some were shy, others bold, some always moving, while certain heavier, lazier ones preferred to lie in the field and daydream. As she petted them and talked with them, she was studying them for their imperfections and any sign that they might need attention. Raising sheep was simple in many ways, and yet many things could go wrong.

She also kept her eye on those she would choose later to exhibit at the County and State Fairs. She knew the guide book by heart: The Suffolk ram with its black face must be rugged with strong bone structure, and the same qualifications held for the ewes, although they should be more refined in their features. She also studied her flock to see which sheep would be most easily handled in the trying circumstances of being judged and which would prove to be most difficult.

"Guess what, everybody! The man with the shears will be here in another week to help you take off your winter coat. Then you'll be ready for a good, long summer."

She liked making all the decisions that were necessary if she were to build the first-rate collection of prize animals, which was one of her dreams. It was all worth it, the daily attentions that must be paid, for that grand moment when she stood in the ring with her sheep while the judges considered their virtues and the sheep ranchers sat in the ring, watching. It hurt only when a sheep that she sold would soon be slaughtered.

She jumped over the fence and exercised the sheep, running with them. Then she brought them their feed and left them to go to the house and have her own breakfast.

A delicious fragrance wafted out from the kitchen. Boysenberry muffins! Her mother knew well that these were Jen's favorites and

here she was making them, most likely thinking her daughter might still be feeling blue
because she had missed the Prom. Jen hugged
her mother good morning.

"I see you're smiling," her mother said.

Jennifer grinned but would not say a word
until all the family were sitting around the
square, wooden kitchen table.

"I've got news," she said. "Bonnie Lass had
a bull calf."

"I wish I'd a been there. Why didn't you
take me, Jen?" Bruce said, clearly disappointed. "Russ said he'd let me watch."

"His timing was off. Anyway, I'm going
over there this morning. Want to come with
me?" Jennifer asked and Bruce's face lit up.
Russ was his hero. Someday he, too, would
have a herd of cows, but at the moment he
had to be content raising a flock of chickens.

"It's great, all that about the calf, but if it
was me, I'd rather have gone to the Prom,"
Terry said.

"You should say 'if it *were* me,' not 'if it *was*
me,'" Jennifer said sternly, not that she
particularly cared about correcting Terry's
grammar, but the remark annoyed her considerably, throwing a small cloud over her
mood. She must not resent it and yet simply
thinking of it could irritate her. She buttered
another muffin and bit savagely into it.

It also worried her that she and Russ had
parted with a certain detachment. She must
make up for it instantly and she would.

When the kitchen was cleared at last,
Jennifer went upstairs to get her camera, a

delightful and expensive little Canon, which fit easily into the palm of her hand and took the sharply delineated photos she admired. She had paid for the camera herself and although Mrs. Cowles had protested over the expense, Jennifer was surprised that her father came to her defense. "She earned the price of it because she raises good lambs," he had said, "and besides, it's a professional expense. She needs pictures of her animals, the finest and clearest she can get."

"Are you ready, Bruce?" Then, not wanting Terry to be left out, she invited her sister, who simply tossed her head.

"I've seen cows and calves before," she said with her nose in the air. She was the rebel, the one who had dropped out of 4-H after one experience with a sewing project. She had other things in mind, such as acting and dancing.

Jennifer and Bruce bicycled to the Steele ranch and as they approached the barn, they saw Russ coming toward them.

"Well, what a surprise! Did you come to see Rex? How's it going, Bruce? Jen?"

He patted Bruce on the shoulder but his eyes sought Jen's questioningly. He can be so charming, but he can also be closed up, secretive; he will never say what he feels. His eyes meeting hers asked the indecisive question, what's going to happen to us? Where are we now? But Bruce was there; everything must seem natural between them.

"Would you like some pictures, Russ?"

"Terrific, Jen. Sure. Want to come, Bruce?"

Jennifer found Bonnie Lass taking her motherhood in stride, turning to lick her son's clean brown and white skin. While Jen took pictures, Russ talked with Bruce.

"And look who's here!" Mrs. Steele said as she came into the barn, put her hand on Bruce's curly head, and said hello to Jen.

"Think we ought to have a special dinner in honor of Rex?" she asked. "I'd like to invite you both."

"Can we, Jen?" Bruce asked with a burst of enthusiasm.

"I hope you'll both come. Fantastic dinner. Barbecued beef, strawberry shortcake, eh, Mom?" Russ said, but Jennifer hesitated.

"My mother's building a new support for the garden, a new way of growing pole beans, and I promised to help her, but thanks anyway."

Why did she say that, she wondered, for although her mother had said something vague about remodeling the garden, surely there was no hurry about it.

"Anyway, I can't wait to develop these pictures," Jennifer added as if needing another excuse.

Russ walked with Jennifer and Bruce down to the gate; he made a friendly fist and punched Bruce's arm, a sign of masculine understanding, but again his eyes met Jennifer's, imploring an answer to the question he could not ask.

"Don't forget we have a meeting tonight at Guerrero's. I'll call for you in the pickup about seven. Okay?"

"Of course." She wished that he would take her in his arms and kiss her, holding her close to reassure her they were still together. Would he have done this were Bruce not there?

They rode away on their bicycles, yet before turning on the curve in the road that would block the view, Jennifer looked back and saw that Russell, standing at the gate, was following her with his eyes. She waved and then disappeared from his view.

Her mother was bending down, weeding the sprouts of crabgrass and thistle that persisted in coming up between the rows of seedlings. When she saw Jennifer she stood up, perhaps a little more slowly than usual (or had Jennifer never noticed before that from time to time her mother appeared a trifle weary?).

"How's the new calf? Did you get some good pictures?"

"I think so. I can't wait to develop them and see, but I thought you'd want some help in the garden."

"If you would be so kind, Jen! I'm swamped. I can't even begin that new support today. I want to transplant some squash, set out snail bait, string up the peas, and place the wire frames around the tomatoes. And then if there's time . . ."

"That alone will take a week, Mom!"

As Jennifer bent down to begin pulling the grass, thistle, and dandelion that appeared so innocent now, but would become an enemy if allowed to grow, she began to think about gardening. An endless task, it was the same every year. You prepared the ground, dug it up, spread compost and manure over it. You planted seeds that had been carefully raised in flats and you took care of the constant enemies: an endless parade of snails, slugs, and insects. If a plant survived, it was likely that a dog running through the garden would flatten it in a matter of moments. In the fall you had to pull up the dead stems, bury them, and begin the winter garden.

"Why do you do it, Mom?"

"Do what?"

"Garden every year. Most ranch women simply go to the store and buy what they need. You've got enough work without this, too."

"For one thing, our fruits and vegetables are far better and fresher than anything you'd get in a store. You never know what chemicals and sprays are used on commercial produce and the food isn't as freshly picked as ours is. Besides, it's expensive to buy food."

"But it's so much work. You always have such a big garden."

"Did you ever think that maybe I like it?"

"Sure. And you win prizes at the fairs and all that. But . . . but there's more than one way to live. Don't you ever feel that you'd like to stop working and just lie down with a good story, or just sun yourself all day long?"

Mrs. Cowles laughed. "It crosses my mind and once in a while I do just that. And I insist on my four o'clock break. But as for giving up the garden, I couldn't, because it feels right for me to be here. You might call it a vocation, if that's not too fancy a word."

They worked in silence for the next twenty minutes, Mrs. Cowles humming as she planted bean seedlings.

"It's a little like your sheep, Jennifer. Nobody makes you do it. It's work. But don't you feel that it's your thing?"

"Sure, Mom, I guess so."

Yet as Jennifer pulled up a particularly nasty little piece of thistle that, young as it was, pricked her unkindly, she began to wonder if one couldn't make choices. She had always lived on a ranch and she could not imagine *not* raising sheep or living in a place where there was no garden, demanding as the garden was. But now it was not so much doubt but curiosity that tagged along behind her, catching at the heels of her thoughts.

"Jen, don't you have a paper due at school on Monday? If you're going out tonight . . ."

Jennifer showered, then sat at her desk while the kittens crawled over her, posing on her shoulders, kneading her hair, until she caught them, held them close, and then released them. "I can't play now. Don't you know that?"

She gathered her notes and began to write, but she couldn't concentrate. Scenes from the T.V. drama she had seen the night before kept jumping into her mind. She saw herself driving with five new glamorous friends, imagined herself stretched out on the white sands of the beach while the sun beat down, and she had nothing more demanding to do than let herself become tanned. No family cow to milk, no sheep to be taken care of, no little bummer lamb to trot after her wanting to be fed every two hours, no garden to weed, no summer days to be spent gathering vegetables and freezing them or canning them for the next winter's food supply. What heaven that would be!

The point of her pencil snapped off, a good excuse to go downstairs to sharpen it. A few minutes after four and she still had so much to do! Yet, she paused in the doorway of the kitchen as she saw her mother indulging in her "four o'clock," which was reserved for a cup of hot tea and a glance at a magazine. But this time, instead of reading she gazed out of the window at the green, rolling hills. On one of them Jennifer's brother was plowing even rows in the rich brown earth with his tractor. The sheep were grazing in the pasture, the lambs following their mothers, while in another pasture the cow lay dreaming, chewing her cud. Mrs. Cowles may well have been daydreaming herself, the inner private thoughts she would never impart to anyone. In the long run, although people lived with each other, even as mother and daughter, each had a secret life.

Jennifer felt a rush of love for her mother, and surprised her with a kiss on the back of her neck.

"What a surprise, Jen! Thank you, darling. How about a cup of hot tea."

"Well, why not? Anything to keep from attacking that dreadful paper."

As she went to pour tea for herself, Bruce rushed in, dropped the day's mail in front of his mother, grabbed three cookies, and disappeared outdoors again.

Mrs. Cowles looked through the envelopes, advertisements, bills, and bank statements, then she let out a cry of delight as she held up a lavender envelope on which her name and address was penned in violet ink in bold upright letters.

"At last! Word from Lois!" she cried.

4.

"Well, what do you know! I haven't heard from my sister for at least two years. Only Christmas and birthday cards."

"What does she say, Mom?"

"Well, she's married again."

"So, what else is new? Is this the third or fourth time? I lose count."

"The fourth, I think. This one, Ted Graham, is an engineer. Used to be in Los Angeles, but they've moved north . . . doesn't say exactly where . . . about twenty-five miles north of San Francisco. One of those suburbs, I suppose."

"Maybe we can go."

"It would be between 150 and 200 miles, I think. With all we have to do, to say nothing of the price of gas, we won't be going there very often. Doesn't mention her address. Or telephone."

"Does she say anything about Margo?"

"Only that she thinks the move was probably a good idea." Mrs. Cowles glanced at the letter again. "She sends her love and says she'll see us one of these days. Love, Lois. And that's that."

34

"I wonder if Margo will come after what happened last time. I was pretty bad, wasn't I, Mom?"

"Yes, you were awful but I don't blame you."

Terry came in, collapsed on a kitchen chair, face hot after a long bicycle ride. "I'm dying. Can I have a drink of juice or something? What did Jen do that was so awful?"

Jennifer gave her sister a glass of milk, and poured another cup of tea for her mother.

"Your Aunt Lois came to visit us once, when Margo and Jennifer were ten years old. Margo kept making nasty remarks about Jen's chickens, how dumb they were, how they smelled, how stupid they sounded."

"I was only trying to show them off because they were my 4-H project and they were good birds. There was a bucket of mash right there by the door, so I picked it up and dumped it on her head. I just couldn't resist."

"Margo howled as if she'd been murdered. She was wearing a pretty dress, and she bawled that it was ruined, and everyone was upset. I was angry, too, because mash was so expensive and I was afraid Lois would never come again."

"And she hasn't. But, I can't imagine she's still angry."

"No, Lois never bore grudges. I think she'll come."

"You mean, Aunt Lois, the actress, is going to come here?" Terry asked, eyes wide.

"You must never call her 'Aunt Lois,'" Jennifer warned. She then imitated her aunt,

35

catching her charm as she pressed her hand to her cheek. " 'Jennifer, *darling*, if you don't mind, you mustn't call me "aunt." It makes me feel a hundred years old, at least. Just Lois.' I thought that was great, being told to call a grownup by her first name."

"And I've never even met her," Terry moaned. "I was spending that day with Katie Hollister. Did she say when she's going to come, Mom?"

"Lois never mentions details like that."

"Do you think she can do something for me, like get me into the movies or T.V.?"

"H'mmm. I don't imagine she's been doing much acting, but you can ask."

"She's been too busy getting married and divorced and married and divorced. Mom, I don't know how people can do that."

"It happens all the time," Terry said. "Even around here."

"Well, yes, but not so much. Anyway, we can't judge because we don't know the details," Mrs. Cowles said in a conciliatory way. "And now, if we're going to get dinner ready, we'd better start. Terry, would you like to make custards? I'll take care of the stew. Jennifer, you make the salad."

Ordinarily the sisters would have made excuses about doing something else, but this time Terry had to hear all the old, familiar stories about her rebellious aunt. Even Bruce, wandering through the kitchen with a basket of eggs he had just collected, sat on the floor and played with the kittens as he listened.

"There's not much to tell," Mrs. Cowles said. "We grew up in a small town in Iowa. Snow White and Rose Red. I always liked gardening and had an eye out for the country. Lois had a touch of wildness in her. Couldn't wait to get away. On the day she graduated from high school, she ran off to Chicago to join a theater group there. She nearly starved. Then she went to New York and nearly starved there, but she did get a few parts. Then it was Hollywood, and a few parts there, and a few marriages. Terry, you're dropping eggshells in the custard."

Jennifer, listening to the familiar anecdotes, wondered if patterns repeated themselves. Was it ordained that she, who so resembled her mother, would spend her life here in the Valley on this ranch or on one of her own, and that Terry would run off as soon as she could? That appeared to be the pattern. But did it have to be that way? She pulled a head of lettuce apart with unexpected savagery. What if *she*, rather than Terry, decided to take off? Just for a little while, she assured herself. Still, where would she go? What would she do?

It's nonsense to think about it, she decided, tearing the lettuce more gently, and mixing the oil and vinegar with herbs, as if these common duties would calm her. And yet the excitement was mounting. Someone, in particular her aunt, her glamorous Aunt Lois, would be coming to visit soon, bringing with her a touch of the outside world.

* * *

If Jennifer dismissed her disturbance as so much nonsense, Russ recognized that something was happening. He had taken her to the meeting that night. She had helped make summer plans with even more enthusiasm than usual, as if she were willing the coming summer, with its picnics, its money-raising events, its plans for a strawberry festival and special classes in showmanship, to be the best ever. She had smiled too much, had laughed too quickly, had declared they would make it a summer to remember.

The night was velvety black as Russ drove her over the softly rolling hills of the Valley toward home, but instead of going there directly, he parked by a grove of eucalyptus trees. Their pungent odor penetrated the clear night air.

"Okay, Jennifer, will you tell me what's going on?"

"What do you mean, what's going on? I'm not sure I like the way you said that. I don't even know what you're talking about."

"I wish I could explain," he said so sweetly that Jennifer immediately regretted her tone of voice. He was trying very hard to analyze what he meant. "Tonight at the meeting you were full of ideas and energy, more than usual, but it was almost too much, as if you were forcing yourself to see that *we would have the best summer ever.*" He emphasized his speech to show that she had almost made it mandatory that this should be so.

"Don't you think we should try to have a good summer?"

"Sure. But not with a wham, pow, yeah, rah rah. If you know what I mean. Something else is going on. I can feel it in you."

She shrugged her shoulders. If she couldn't explain to herself her restlessness, in spite of her very real contentment at living here in the Valley, how could she explain it to anyone, Russ most of all!

"I've been wondering," he was stumbling now as he picked his way among the words, an unusual role for him. "If maybe there's someone else you like and if that's what's wrong. If there is, you should tell me. We have to be honest with each other, Jen."

So he was human, and suffering jealousy. Oddly enough this delighted her; perhaps he did care for her, but then again it might only be bruised ego.

"Maybe there is and maybe there isn't," she said to tantalize him, but then he appeared so woebegone that she laughed and put her hand on his cheek. "Of course not, Russ. So stop worrying."

"That's good," he said, but instead of telling her that he loved her, which was what she wanted to hear, he went back to his original question. "If it's not that, what is it, Jennifer?"

"Nothing. It's NOTHING."

"You're not upset because of the Prom?"

"Please, Russ. For the last time. *I understand.* Anyway, it's over."

Then she rapidly changed the subject in order to avoid any more discussion. "I almost forgot to tell you. My Aunt Lois is coming to see us. Maybe Margo will come too."

"The Margo that you anointed with chicken mash?" He knew the story. He smiled.

"I hope she comes, but it's really my aunt I want to see. Only I'm not supposed to call her 'aunt.' She was so beautiful and so different."

"So different from what? You can't just be different; it's a comparative term."

"You're such a purist, Russ! She's different from . . . from the rest of us, at least from all the other women I know. She comes from another kind of life."

"I suppose so."

"Sometimes, I feel as if I were living on an island, a dry island, of course, landlocked, just a tiny part of a very large world. When Lois comes, she'll bring a little of that world with her. I find it exciting."

"And I find this island . . . calling the Central Valley an island is the most ridiculous thing I've ever heard, but I know what you mean. I find our ranch and the life around it a whole universe. We're always dealing with life and death, trying to understand all those things that constantly baffle us, like an animal getting sick without apparent cause or a crop doing well one year and suffering the next. To me it's beautiful because it's real."

"I think so, too, Russ. Like this night, the

air, the way the leaves rustle. Only sometimes I wonder about what's out there."

"All you have to do is get in your car and drive out and see."

"It's not that simple." She didn't want to explain that the Cowles' finances didn't allow much in the way of vacation and her own funds were strictly earmarked for college and could not be touched.

Russ put his arm around her and whispered. "Don't go too far away, will you, Jen? Don't stay away too long. Okay?"

At one time she would have taken this as an expression of love. Now she saw it as a promise he wanted her to make. Don't promise anything, a voice cried out to her with panic force. The next moment, she laughed it off.

"Russ, this is so silly. It's not as if I were on my way somewhere. Not a prospect in sight. Just dreaming. Don't worry."

He embraced her and she thought how good it was to be in his arms. But it was also like Russ to break it off. "Do you know, I have a paper to finish before I go to sleep tonight. I'm sorry, Jen, I have to get back."

"And I'll be up to two a.m. myself," she said. He drove her home and without lingering went on to the Steele Ranch. Life was normal once more. Everything would be all right. Or so she thought.

5.

"When is she gonna come? Why do we have to be so far away from everything?" Terry moaned.

"Patience, Terry! If Lois says she's going to come, she'll come. Just wait. She won't let us know ahead of time, but will simply drop in one day when I'm in my grubbiest old jeans, cleaning out the chicken coop, while she'll be wearing some trifle whipped up by a French designer. It's sure to happen," Mrs. Cowles said without rancor.

"Oh, Mom, it's not like you to have such rotten luck."

Mrs. Cowles laughed. "It's not really such rotten luck. I'm always glad to see that wild sister of mine. It's just that she has the talent for dropping in when she's least expected."

At first Jennifer, like Terry, could hardly wait to see her aunt and cousin, but as spring came, bringing days crowded with things to be done at home, as well as at school, Lois and Margo dropped out of her mind. The disturbing restlessness she had experienced around the time of the Prom subsided as she prepared for exhibitions, took part in a gymnastics meet at the high school, went with Russ to several high schools to give talks about 4-H, and was invited to any number of birthdays celebrated by slumber parties. She was too busy to ask herself if she were content with her life.

Then one day in May, as the schoolbus let her off, she saw something red behind the trees near the house and coming closer saw it was a Triumph. "Oh, you darling car!" she cried. A car made for romance and the carefree life. But whose car was it? It burst on her at once.

Lois had come!

At one time Jennifer would have burst straight into the living room to embrace her aunt, but now she stopped in front of the hall mirror. Her face glowed red with early sunburn, and her hair could do with a good brushing. She wished she had worn her new T shirt instead of this ordinary white shirt, but it was too late to change now.

"Jennifer? Come in and see Lois and Margo," her mother called.

Her aunt was sitting in the flowered wing chair, poised and serene, exactly what one would expect of a stage personality. At first glance, Jennifer found her as lovely as she remembered her, the dark hair drawn back dramatically, the lively, deep eyes wide and brilliant, the smile open. She wore a stylish blouse of purple gauze over pants of oyster silk, rose-colored sandals, a glimmer of gold jewelry, a quick scent of an exotic perfume, and an oversized straw bag, which rested at her feet. She could have been photographed exactly as she was, and Jennifer wished she had her camera for just such a portrait.

"Jennifer, is that you? Can you have grown so?"

Even the voice sounded the same, low and melodious, the voice of an actress, artificial but beautiful in its huskiness. Lois stood up and Jennifer rushed over to embrace her.

"Aunt Lois — I mean, Lois . . . it's wonderful to see you. You're just the same. Really beautiful."

"Am I really? But you're not the same, Jennifer. You were a little girl when I saw you last and now you're growing up. What an amazing beauty! Emily, this is exactly how you looked when you were sixteen. Jen, are all the boys after you the way they ran after your mother?"

"Why, Mom, you never told me that," Jennifer said. "Secrets?"

"I'll tell you all about it," Lois said. "Your mother was . . . and still is . . . a gorgeous lady. It's you I can't get over. I suppose I expected you to remain a freckle-faced little girl with braids forever. Your freckles are gone, and look at that marvelous hair, you lucky girl."

Jennifer, embarrassed at such a blatant compliment asked, "Is Margo here?"

"Yes. Terry is showing her through the house. She'll be down soon, I guess. Your mother has been telling me all about you, your ribbons and medals, your sheep, your prizes, and just about everything else. I can't get over it. It's wonderful to see you so . . ." The shoulders rose and fell. "So full of life."

"I'm afraid Mom exaggerates. Really, it's nothing out of the ordinary."

Lois interrupted. "Here's Margo now with that gorgeous sister of yours."

Margo's the one who's changed, Jennifer thought as she turned around to greet her cousin. So pretty, a certain pixie quality in the faintly slanted, green eyes and dark lashes, the black hair that curled like tendrils around her heart-shaped face. She reminded Jennifer of a colt, a well-bred, sensitive creature that had yet to be proven. Still, she hung back, lacking her mother's enthusiasm.

"Margo, you remember Jennifer, don't you?"

"Of course. I could never forget her. Hello."

The "hello" was so cool that Jennifer thought, oh dear, she has probably not forgotten the unfortunate episode with the chicken mash. Later, she would apologize, but not now.

"I'm glad to see you, Margo. How do you like living up north?"

"It's all right, I suppose. Not at all like Los Angeles. That would be too much to expect, but we're only twenty miles from San Francisco, so it could be worse. I mean, we could be farther away. Hillside's okay, I guess."

"I've heard of Hillside, but I've never been there," Jennifer said.

"Well, you'll not only be hearing about it,

all of you will have to come and see it, as soon as we settle in. It's not far at all," Lois said.

"Lois, are you acting in any plays now? I'd love to see you on the stage. I'd be so proud," Terry said.

Lois threw her head back and laughed. "My darling, I haven't been on the stage for . . . for a very long time. But I couldn't live without the theater. It's my life."

"It's my life, too. I love acting. And dancing. There's nothing else I'd rather do," Terry said, sighing and seating herself theatrically at her aunt's feet.

"Terry's been showing us upstairs," Margo said, "and your mother showed us all your ribbons and everything. And that pink evening gown. It's beautiful, considering it's homemade."

"Mother!" Jennifer was upset with her mother, and apparently Lois was not entirely pleased with her daughter as she scolded her.

"That wasn't the nicest remark, Margo. The dress is truly beautiful, Jennifer. It has the appearance that French designers strive for, a dress made by skillful hands, for one person only. A work of art, really, I mean it."

"Thanks, Lois, that's really putting it on."

Mrs. Cowles changed the subject.

"You and Margo will have dinner with us, won't you? Bill will want to see you and I think Ken may be coming, too."

"But we've just had such a lovely tea." Lois could sound English when she wished. Nobody ever said "a lovely tea" in Grant.

"Please stay, please," Terry begged, and Jennifer added that she would love it if they did.

"In that case, we'll take you up on it," Lois said. "It's such a treat to be here in this wonderful old house. It's a real gem. And we haven't seen you for such a long time. But you must let us help. What can I do?"

"Nothing," Mrs. Cowles said. "Remember the time we made dinner for the minister . . ."

"And you made that high five-layer cake and the top layer slid off and the second one collapsed and finally we had to serve it all up in dessert dishes . . ."

And so the sisters were off telling stories, and the three girls listened. At the same time, Jennifer compared the two sisters. It was incredible that they had been born of the same parents and brought up in the same house, and yet not only looked so different but had taken opposite paths. Lois, who had been the wild one, now appeared so young and vivacious she could have been taken for Margo's older sister. Yet Emily, Jennifer's mother, the good daughter who had stayed at home and held a job as a teacher, looked her forty-three years, a hard-working woman in a worn cotton shirt and denim skirt, her face lined with the dryness that ranch women are prone to when they've been in the sun too long.

But as the stories poured out, it was clear they shared an intimacy that differed from that of even good friends. Though adults now, Jennifer could almost sense them as children growing up together. Lois imitated characters they had known vividly, and Jennifer's mother came up with some striking dramatizations herself. But their chatter and laughter was being interrupted by a more and more incessant mooing from Queen Bess, the family cow, and Jennifer knew how her mother was caught between the need to milk Bess and the reluctance to leave Lois.

"Mom, you stay here. I'll take care of Bess," Jennifer said.

"Would you mind, Jen? I do love every moment I can get with my little sister."

The "little sister" smiled. "She couldn't enjoy it any more than I do."

To Jennifer's surprise, Margo followed her out to the barn. She stood back and watched while Jennifer cleaned the milking pail and sat on the stool, her head resting against Queen Bess' pale flanks as she milked her.

"You really surprise me," Margo said at last. "I didn't think you'd turn out to be so good-looking. I always thought of you as a nasty little girl with pigtails and a temper."

"And I thought you were a stuck-up ignoramus. I did have a nasty temper," Jennifer confessed. "I guess when you're ten, your opinions shouldn't be taken seriously forever."

"Sure," Margo laughed. "We may as well forget it."

"Of course," Jennifer said. "I'd like to be real friends. If you don't mind my saying so, I'm amazed at how really beautiful you are. You seemed all legs and braces then. But now, you could be a model. Would you want to be an actress like your mother?"

"Not in the least," Margo said slowly and deliberately. "In no way at all, do I want to be anything like my mother."

"Oh I see!" Jennifer said tactfully, turning back to pay attention to the milk that squirted into the pail. Apparently, some kind of conflict was going on between mother and daughter. She had seen this happen often enough among the girls she knew, so she expected it was perhaps natural, yet she had never crossed swords with her own mother. Maybe they had too much to do. Margo changed the subject abruptly.

"Jennifer, who's the boyfriend? He's darling."

"Boyfriend? Who do you mean?"

"You know. That one with the western hat. You have a large photograph of him on the wall in your room. Russell someone."

"Oh sure, Russell Steele. Well, that's one of the few good portraits I've taken after rolls and rolls of film. So I had it enlarged. That's all."

"You're not talking? Tell me, is he your lover?"

Jennifer stopped milking, the term so astonished her when applied to Russ and herself. She recovered quickly enough and tossed off her answer, hoping Margo wouldn't think her a naive country girl. "My *lover*? No. We're just friends. We work together in 4-H. He's always been our neighbor, so there's nothing very personal about it."

"That's not what Terry says. She says you are always going over there, or he's calling you, or coming over here, and that he gave you your first lamb, a real expensive lamb."

"Lucky for me! That was Loulou, my first lamb, a bummer. That means her mother had died and someone had to bring her up, giving her bottles of milk every few hours. It's a lot of work and Russ didn't have time for it. Loulou comes of good stock; she's the mother of my herd. After she came, I became really interested in raising sheep. But I guess you find that dull."

"It's what you leave out that fascinates me. About you and Russ."

"Sorry I can't make it more interesting. Let's talk about you. I'll bet you have hundreds of boys following around after you."

"A few," Margo said modestly. Then her voice became spirited. "There's one guy I've met recently. Fabulous. Really, I've never known anyone like him in all my life."

Jennifer, surprised at the enthusiasm in her cousin's voice, looked up.

"What's he like?"

"Oh, Jennifer, if only I could tell you. He's what I consider the ultimate in masculinity. He's handsome, fearless, bold, sophisticated. Unfortunately, he'll be graduating, so next year he'll be away while I'll still be in Hillside. He's not your average high school boy, I tell you. He's . . . he's fantastic."

Jennifer stopped milking. "You sound as if you were really in love."

"Maybe I am. Maybe I'm not. So many girls

are after him. Everyone in the club is crazy about him. We call it LaClique."

"Oh, a French club? What do you do?"

"Well, I don't imagine it's like 4-H," Margo said, a snide remark, but Jennifer let it pass since Margo appeared to want her friendship. "There are sixteen of us who get together. We don't let just anyone in because we all understand each other very well and we want to keep it that way."

"There, good girl, Bess!" Jennifer interrupted, for she had extracted the last drop from Queen Bess' udders. Margo, talking of the informal parties and games and picnics LaClique enjoyed, walked beside her cousin, watched her pour the steaming milk into a tall metal milk can and place it in a cooler. She followed Jennifer as she put down some hay for Queen Bess and stopped to pet Fuzzy, the latest bummer to have adopted Jennifer as a mother.

Margo's a watcher and I'm a doer, Jennifer was thinking as she rinsed out the milk pail and set it on the boards to dry. Lucky Margo! As Margo described a beach party LaClique had held the previous Sunday, the T.V. drama that had taken such a hold on Jennifer once more flickered through her mind. Margo's life would be filled with pleasure because she was so flowerlike, so inviting. She would sail through college without studying, and bad grades wouldn't matter because she would be sure to get along one way or another, cadge a good job, have to work hard, or find herself a wealthy husband. She, Jennifer, would do well, but not through luck. She would have to work for every gain made.

"I guess we're finished," Jennifer said lightly. As they walked back to the kitchen she noticed how well her cousin's jeans fit around her trim hips; a neat bit of stitching spelled out *N'est-ce pas* on the back pocket. Jennifer wondered what it would be like to own such well-tailored pants and to belong to an exclusive club with a French name. Not that I'm jealous, she told herself, only curious.

Everyone was working in the kitchen. Lois, laughing and telling stories as she sipped a glass of sherry, somehow managed to wash a head of lettuce for the salad while Jennifer's mother prepared a casserole, scrubbed potatoes for baking, and whipped biscuits for a luxurious, strawberry shortcake. Bruce, coming in from the yard, was obviously overwhelmed by his pretty cousin who flattered him skillfully. And then Jennifer's father and Kenneth walked in. The house sang with the gaiety of an unexpected holiday, and soon everyone was seated around the oval dining room table.

As Mr. Cowles stood up to recite a brief blessing, Jennifer was thinking, I will always remember this day. Her aunt seemed to bring with her a sense of something fresh, a touch of the outer world. Margo, though relatively quiet, basked in the obvious admiration she received from her male cousins. Only once was the pleasant atmosphere broken, when Mrs. Cowles spoke in a voice so low it was scarcely audible to anyone but her sister.

"No more wine, Lois. Not if you're driving tonight."

"Now, don't you worry about me. I can take care of myself." Lois' voice may have been ever so slightly blurred. No more was said about it.

It was nearly nine when she was ready to leave. No, she didn't mind driving at night, she said, not a bit. She thanked her sister a hundred times over, kissed everyone good-night, and then, just before getting in the car, took Jennifer aside and whispered in her ear. "You're going to get a letter from me one of these days and I want you to think about it very seriously."

"Really? What's going to be in that letter?"

Lois raised a finger to her lip. "A secret. You'll find out later."

And then everyone was standing around as Lois and Margo got into the smart, little red car, adjusted their seat buckles, and waved good-bye as the car started easily, and then disappeared as it sped down the country road.

"A special day," she wrote in her diary. She had been given a glimpse of a world that was nothing like her own, that mysterious, outside world. She was alone in her bedroom again, with studying to be done for a chemistry exam, and yet she kept seeing her aunt and cousin waving good-bye as they left the Cowles' ranch and she stayed behind.

6.

What did her aunt want to tell her? For two days the mystery of it haunted Jennifer. To divulge a family secret? Some kind of personal confidence? An offer to go on the stage? Nonsense, she was becoming as silly as Terry. After five days when no letter came, Jennifer snapped her fingers, easy come, easy go. Most likely Lois had forgotten all about it.

Besides, life was much too busy. There was no time for dreaming.

"Oh, Russ, I wish we could take the horses today and just go riding. A long, long ride over the hills. Maybe to Lawson Creek. The weather's so perfect. By the time school's out, it will be too hot."

"Wish we could go, Jen. But I've got something to do. Are you entering the essay contest?"

"Sure. Guess I'd better," Jennifer said. A cash prize would help her college fund. "And when I'm through with that, I have to fix the fence around the lambing pen. And my mom's got so much work in the garden . . ."

She refused to complain of the pressure of

work, for her father often spent ten or twelve hours a day or more, even when Kenneth took off time from his own job to come and help out. To make matters worse, Aunt Annie, her father's sister who lived in a farming community near Clear Lake, became ill and Mrs. Cowles had to go and take care of her. This meant that Jennifer had to take care of the house and garden in addition to everything else. It would be for only a week but it seemed to last forever.

"I don't know why I have to make dinner tonight," Terry complained. "It's hot and Kathy Graham invited me over to her house to go swimming."

"We're all taking turns and it's fair," Jennifer said sternly. "Everyone works equally hard and you're the only one who grumbles."

If only she had her mother's sweet temper. . . .

"You just aren't listening. Everyone's complaining," Terry said pointedly.

"Tough. We ought to be thankful for everything we've got. Anyway, this won't last forever. Come on, Terry, I've got work to do, too. I'll help you, so stop making such an issue over it. Cheer up, okay?"

"You're beginning to sound just like Mother, Jen. Everything is for the best and we should all be grateful. Sometimes I wish she would just stand there and scream, it would be such a relief. You scream enough."

"I certainly don't. Do I?"

"Well, no. Actually you're always beaming,

like that girl on the calendar in the kitchen, the one who's drinking milk. So cheerful, it makes me want to throw up."

"Well, thanks a lot. I lose either way. Now c'mon, Terry, *let's make dinner*."

"Later," she said, skipping out the back door.

Jennifer uttered a forbidden four-letter word and began to make the dinner. Tears streamed down her cheeks as she sliced the onions in thin perfect rounds.

Too cheerful? Not today, sister. Would her life be like this forever and forever? Would she become like her mother: controlled, hard-working, never permitting herself a holiday or a complaint?

And yet, three days later when her mother did come home, Terry could not do enough to help Jennifer in preparing an especially delectable dinner.

"It's so good to see you all again!" Grim as her mother's life might appear from time to time, there was no mistaking the real love everyone showed so openly on her return and she, too, was happy to be back.

The very next day a letter arrived from Lois, but it was addressed to Mrs. Cowles, not Jennifer, who bore the disappointment quietly. Mrs. Cowles tore open the envelope, read the letter quickly, and shoved it back.

"What did she say?" Terry asked.

"She thanked us for dinner and said we were a wonderful family."

"Sure we are. But is that all she wrote, Mom?"

Mrs. Cowles appeared preoccupied all day, and it wasn't until later that night, when Jennifer, dressed in a thin cotton nightgown, sat at her desk studying, that her mother knocked and came in. "Jennifer, can we talk for a few minutes?"

"Sure, Mom. Take the chair."

She jumped up to the bed and sat there while her mother thoughtfully tapped the lavender envelope on the desk.

"Your aunt says that she wants to invite you to spend the summer with your new uncle, Margo, and herself."

"That's fantastic. Can I go?"

"Well, she wants our permission before she invites you, which is very thoughtful of her."

"Of course, you'll let me go, won't you?"

"I don't know. I've been wondering about a number of things. You've been looking forward to exhibiting some of your sheep and you'd have to be around for that. And you were going to enter some photographs at the County Fair, weren't you? You might not want to give that all up."

"Oh, Mom, I know, but I've always done those kinds of things."

"There's another matter. I've always depended on your help, but I'd never let it stand in the way of your happiness. You're only sixteen once and I think you deserve a real vacation. So that's in your favor."

"Mom, you're wonderful. But what's bothering you?"

"Your father doesn't think it's a good idea for you to go."

"I don't understand it. Why not?"

"He's not sure you'd be happy there. Nor am I."

"But they live in this beautiful condominium. Lois was talking about it, remember? And we'd go to San Francisco to see plays and Margo would introduce me to her friends . . . oh, Mom, it's everything."

"But your way of living is so different from theirs. I'm not sure Margo would . . . well, *understand* you."

"We'd be good friends. We got on fine the other day. Let's go down and talk with Dad and get it all out in the open."

Her mother agreed. They went downstairs to the porch where Mr. Cowles sat back in the chair as he looked over the fields. What thoughts he had, he kept to himself.

"Dad, Aunt Lois has invited me to stay with her this summer and I want to go. All right?"

"No, Jen, it's not all right."

"But why?"

"Because life down there isn't your life. I believe they call it 'lifestyle.' It will give you illusions. It might also make you unhappy."

"Dad, you're not making sense. How could it make me unhappy? As for illusions, I have a head on my shoulders. Do you think I'd go wild just because I'm away from home?"

"Jennifer, if a man ever trusted his daughter more than me, I'd like to meet him. You've never been really tried before. Living with people who are well off, people who believe

58

in a constant round of pleasure . . . well, it's hard to say just what this would do to you."

"It would be better for me to go and find out now, then stay home forever and always wonder about it," Jennifer said quietly and Mrs. Cowles stepped in.

"That's exactly right, Bill. I trust Jennifer implicitly for good sense, for balance, for knowing what she's been taught."

"And if she doesn't want to come back to the ranch?" Mr. Cowles asked.

"Dad, that would never happen," Jennifer said. "Please let me go. I'll be in touch with you all the time. I'll write. I'll phone. You know, reach out, touch a friend."

Mrs. Cowles put her hand on her husband's shoulder. "It's not easy to see your daughter go, is it, Bill, but it would be worse to demand that she stay here. This is part of growing up."

Mr. Cowles studied his daughter for a full minute. Then he took his pipe from his mouth.

"All right," he said at last.

"Now don't say anything until you actually get the invitation from Lois," Mrs. Cowles warned as she licked the envelope that would take her reply to her sister.

"It will take forever," Jennifer moaned, but she had never been more excited. She could not imagine how she would get through the next week but at last the lavender envelope came and this time it was addressed to her. With trembling fingers she read the letter.

"You see, dear Jen, Margo doesn't have a sister or a brother and most likely will never have one, but a cousin can come close, particularly if that cousin is the darling I know you to be. We'll try to make it a good summer for both of you. And so, swooning with delight, as they say in certain novels, I'm grateful that you are coming."

Then, becoming practical, Lois promised she would be going up to Lake Tahoe for a few days in June and would call for her on the way back.

"Oh, Mom, read it! Read it!" Jennifer cried, hugging her mother. "Hold me down, Mom, because I'm so happy, I might just float away."

7.

She must tell Russell before anyone else, nor would the news last until morning. She hopped on her bicycle and rode over to the Steeles'. She peered through the window and saw that Russ was there studying for finals. She thought she could feel the vibrations of his intense concentration.

Instead of ringing the doorbell, for then she would have had to share the news with Mr. and Mrs. Steele, she picked up a few pebbles and threw them at the window. Russ looked up and seeing nothing, returned to his book. She threw a few more pebbles and hid under the window, but Hero, Russ' golden retriever, barked once, and then rushed up to greet Jennifer with a wagging tail. This time Russ stuck his head out of the window.

"What are you doing, Jen? Come in."

She put a finger to her mouth. "Shh," she said, putting her hands on the window sill and hoisting herself. She could have made it without his help but she let him pull her in anyway.

"It's not as if my parents would drive you

away if you came in through the door, front door, back door, side door . . ."

"Or down through the chimney. I know, but I like it better this way for an important reason. What are you studying?"

"Chemistry. As if you didn't know. I guess you have it all down by heart, going out on the night before the exam and all."

"Don't remind me. I'll be up all night with it, but I've got some news and it just won't wait."

"Let me guess. You bought a new lamb?"

"Strike One."

"You've just won the Nobel Prize."

"That goes without saying. One more."

"You've been making cream puffs and you brought one, or more, over for me."

"Oh you wishful thinker, you. Three strikes and you have to pay the penalty."

"Here it is," he said grabbing her and kissing her with a friendly smack.

"Russ, is that a *penalty*, kissing me?"

"Before I die wondering, will you tell me your secrets?"

"O.K. It's very special."

She sat down crosslegged on the Indian rug and, replaying an old childhood game of theirs, he sat down facing her. She beckoned him to lean forward so she could whisper it in his ear. Happiness was making her silly.

"I've been invited to spend the whole summer with my aunt, my uncle, and my cousin in Hillside, near San Francisco."

The smile vanished as Russell drew back.

"You're not serious, are you? You wouldn't leave, would you?"

"Of course I'm going. My aunt wants me there to be with my cousin. She doesn't have any sisters and so a cousin has to do. They live in a condominium with a swimming pool and a hot tub."

Every trace of gaiety had left Russ' face. "Jennifer, you can't go. You know that."

"No, Russ. I'm going to go."

"You can't leave a ranch in summer. That's the busiest time. It's unthinkable. Besides there's the county fair, the state fair, and besides . . ." He was now so upset he got up and actually paced the floor.

"Jennifer, you know how hard your folks work in summer. Ten or twelve hours a day. Sometimes more. How can you leave them?"

"That's the hard part, Russ. But they think perhaps it's a good idea for me to see how other people live and this is my only chance. After all, it's not that far away. Maybe 175 miles or so."

"It might be all right with them, but it's not all right with me," he said, surprising her with his ferocity. "Remember that special honey bee project we were going to launch this summer? That would involve lots of work, setting up experiments, hives, keeping records. You were so eager to do it, so enthusiastic that you got everyone else excited about it. And now you're backing down."

"I know. I'm sorry. But maybe someone else will take my place. Susan Field would be good."

"It's not Susan I want to work with. I want you. And what about all the awards you were going to get? You've worked for them. Are you going to let them go just like that? Don't forget, you need all the money you can get, even if you do have scholarships for college."

"Well . . ." she hesitated. Everything he said was true and sensible. And yet, here was what she'd been waiting for, what she thought of as a "television summer." Now or never. It dismayed her that he dampened her joy, but it pleased her also that it upset him so to have her leave. He was casting about desperately for any excuse to keep her here. If only he would tell her that he loved her, that he needed her, that he could not bear the thought of losing her, then she would promise to stay away only for a short while, a month, perhaps less. He might be capable of convincing her not to go at all.

She stood stock still, waiting for him to speak, but he only stared at her, paced the floor again, and as if making a decision, stopped before her, putting his hands on her shoulders. Would he tell her now what she wanted to hear?

"You're all excited tonight because it sounds romantic. Go ahead if you want, but I don't think you'll like it. What's more, I don't think you'll stay much more than a week or two."

So this was to be a contest of wills, was it? Possibly he was letting her know she was nothing more than his companion in 4-H, the girl who lived up the road, the country girl too simple-minded to know what she was doing.

"Russ, this time I think you're wrong."

"No, I'm not. Don't you ever forget, Jennifer Cowles, that you are a product of a ranch."

"I love the way you put it, as if I were a bundle of hay or a bushel of wheat."

"You put it very well," he said, not without sarcasm. "You aren't going to transplant to a suburb. It will be very hard for you, wait and see."

"That shows how much you know. Really, Russ, some of the most famous politicians, actresses, writers, professors, doctors all come from farms and they 'transplanted' very successfully. So don't be too sure of yourself."

"I still say, you won't like it. You'll never belong."

"Ho ho ho! I know that I can and I will and what's more I'll *love* it. Well, with a sweet send-off like that, I'll leave you to your chemistry. Good night, Russ."

"Hey, Jen . . ."

He caught her as she was about to leave and this time he held her close and pressed a long kiss on her mouth. "Jen, you don't know how much I'll miss you. It won't be the same without you."

It was the closest he could come to telling her how he felt about her. But why couldn't he use the word "love"?

"I've got to go, Russ. I've got to study."

"All right. Maybe you'll change your mind."

She shook her head no. She was determined to go.

"Well, I have to take the pickup to school tomorrow to get some grain in town. Want to come with me?"

"Yes, I'd like to do that."

He offered to bicycle home with her, but she thanked him and said no. He needed time for studying, as did she. He spoke tenderly now, but his words weren't the ones that would make their way into the romance she craved. Nor would they hold her in Grant that summer.

8.

The school year was ending in a whirlwind. The days piled up with astounding speed, and soon Lois would be coming to call for her.

"You act as if you were going to the moon," Terry said. "It's only 165 miles away."

"Actually, it's close to 200 miles," Jennifer reminded her.

Terry's contempt changed to outspoken jealousy. "*I* ought to be going. *I'm* the one who wants to be on the stage."

"Don't worry, Terry. Your turn will come," Mrs. Cowles comforted her, but Terry pouted. Everything took so long.

Though Mrs. Cowles had championed Jennifer's decision to go, she was more upset than she would let anyone know. But Jennifer was aware of her sadness.

"Mom, I'll be gone for only a little while. It's not as if it were the end of the world. If you wanted me to come home, I'd come."

"I know. It's silly of me to feel this way. Somehow it was always all right when you went off to 4-H camp each year, but this is different," Mrs. Cowles confessed.

It was the same fear she had recognized in Russell. Did they think she would change that much or that she would never return?

Russ insisted on being with her every minute that he could.

"Come, let's exercise the horses. How about a long ride?" he begged.

"But, Russ," she answered, surprised, for this was the busiest time of the year, "there's so much work we have to do."

"I know, but I thought you'd like it." And so they would take time off to ride over their favorite trails. Russ found excuses to touch her more often now, holding her close and burying his lips in the sunny blondness of her hair; yet he never once uttered the words she wanted to hear.

Mrs. Steele insisted on making a somewhat formal "gourmet" dinner in Jennifer's honor, inviting all the Cowles to share it. She gave Jennifer a tailored nightgown with embroidered initials.

The 4-H Club put on a year-end bash with a special bouquet for Jennifer. It was the usual party at the Grange Hall.

"I'll miss you all, even if I'll only be away for a little while," she cried.

On the night before she was to leave, her mother made a Special Occasion dinner to which the Steeles were invited. The very best of everything was used, from the embroidered linen tablecloth and the best dishes and silver, to Jennifer's favorite menu. After dinner, a tray of presents was brought in by a grinning Bruce and set before Jennifer.

"It's like a birthday!" she said, wiping away the tears that embarrassed her.

Everyone had found something for her. From Terry: panties with painted kittens, rolls of film, a box of stationery with stamps, and a diary; an envelope of money from her parents, a genuine sacrifice; and at the bottom of the pile a small box wrapped in gold paper.

"Aha, what's this!" she said turning it over.

"Open it! Come on, Jen. Don't tease."

She removed the paper slowly and found a jeweler's box, inside of which rested a gold chain from which dangled a small jade sheep, exquisitely carved.

"Oh, Russ, this is so . . . so perfectly beautiful. I've never seen anything like it."

Then she saw the small note at the bottom of the box. "Don't forget us, Fuzzy, Loulou, and all your lambs."

"You gotta read it out loud."

"What does it say? You can't have any secrets," Terry cried.

Bruce whistled, suggesting a torrid message had been enclosed, but Jennifer just put the note away and Russ sighed in relief.

Then he helped clasp the chain around Jennifer's neck. She raised her blue eyes to him and whispered. "Don't worry, Russ. I couldn't forget Fuzzy or Loulou or anyone here. Not ever. You're all so . . . so dear."

But Terry and Bruce were grinning up at her and hanging on every word, so she made a little face at them and said no more.

* * *

69

On June 20th at four, just as she had promised, Lois drove up in the red Triumph to call for Jennifer. In spite of all the work he had to do, Russ had hung around the Cowles' ranch all day, helping Bruce build a new wing to the chicken house, but for the most part checking to see that Jennifer wasn't whisked away before it was time for her to leave.

Jennifer, spotless in new white pants and a tailored shirt, had long since packed her suitcase. But Mrs. Cowles insisted that Lois have some lemonade before driving any further. Besides, she must meet Russ, who came forward and shook hands with her formally. "So this is Russ!" Lois murmured, obviously impressed.

As they sat around the table in the yard, under a black walnut tree, Jennifer saw how her aunt played up to Russ by flattering him, actually flirting with him as she asked questions about his ranch and his herd of cows, although it was obvious to Jennifer she did not really care. It was ridiculous, a grown woman like that trying to impress him.

Jennifer squirmed uneasily. She saw Russ so much she nearly forgot how attractive he could be. It was possible that in her absence he might easily take up with someone else. Susan, Pat, Linda? They were all pretty. The loving words he couldn't tell her might easily come in the presence of another girl. She might be making a mistake in leaving.

But it was too late to do anything about it

now. Perhaps she would stay for ten days or two weeks, but not the whole summer.

"My goodness, it's five already!" Lois said as she glanced at her tiny, gold watch. "We should leave. Emily, darling, we'll take good care of your gorgeous daughter, believe me. You're a doll to let her go."

Mr. Cowles came in from the field and now everyone stood around for a last-minute embrace. A sudden hubbub of promises to behave, to write, to take care. A blinking of eyes suddenly moist. Somehow Fuzzy knew what was going on and managed to break out of the pen and come trotting up to Jennifer for reassuring pats of love. For a moment Jennifer quivered with consternation; she was leaving behind everything that she loved.

"You'll be back, Jennifer," Russ said, a statement, not a question. He had kissed her the night before with an intensity that had surprised her. For the benefit of everyone now closely watching, he kissed her again quickly before any whistling could be sounded. A good friend kiss.

And then her suitcase was piled in the car along with the flowers and vegetables and jars of jam that Mrs. Cowles insisted on sending along. Although she had been waiting for days and days, in no time at all the red Triumph drove down the narrow driveway to the road, leaving the Cowles Ranch behind.

9.

"It's so beautiful."

Although Jennifer had lived in California all her life, she had seen little of it. As Lois drove down the Redwood Highway, vistas of blue and purple hills with towns and houses tucked among them, the feeling that the Pacific was not far away, brought about an excitement in Jennifer. It was totally unlike the fertile valley where she had always lived, with its gentle hills, its orderly orchards, and carefully tended fields.

"Yes, it's lovely. Too bad the highway is always so crowded with cars, but once we get off you'll see, it can be quiet and easy going. We're not too far from the ocean, not too far from the city. Jen, we're a little late getting home, but even so I'd like to talk with you before we get there and I'd rather not be driving when I do it, so let's stop off."

Jennifer tried not to flinch as Lois passed a truck neatly but too closely in order to take an exit from the freeway. She parked in front of a small restaurant, a pretty place that suggested a cool and dark interior on a blistering summer day. Lois ordered a scotch and soda for herself. Jennifer decided to have an orangeade.

"Really, Jen? Darling, you're not at home. You're with your Auntie Lois and if you want something with a bit of spirit, I'll understand. And I won't tell your mother. How about a nice gin and tonic?"

"No, thanks, Lois. I'd have asked for it if I'd wanted it, but I've decided that drinking isn't for me. I don't smoke either. There, you might just as well know the bad news now," she said lightly.

Lois lifted her eyebrows questioningly. Was there something wrong with her niece?

"It's just that I've made certain decisions about my life. Someday I may change, but at the moment, orangeade suits me fine."

"Well, you do stand by your principles, don't you. I wish Margo had them. Jen, I don't like to talk behind Margo's back, but her life is so different from yours, perhaps a little explanation is in order. You should be warned about her."

"Warned?" Jennifer asked, puzzled.

"Yes, she might not be easy to live with. I can't tell. On the one hand she seems to like you very much and wants you here. She needs a close friend; she does have acquaintances but it's not the same. You might find her spoiled. She's never had to share anything with a brother or sister; she's never had to work. An only child with a succession of fathers can have a difficult time. Not all my husbands have felt kindly about taking on someone else's daughter."

"I just can't imagine what it would be like."

"Sometimes it doesn't seem to bother her at all, but these matters can be treacherous. She has enough boyfriends. What she really needs is a girl friend, someone who's understanding, someone strong."

"Me? Strong? But I have problems, too, Lois. I don't know if I can help her."

"Just be there. That's all you have to do. She can be rebellious. I understand most teenagers are. Somehow I can't imagine that you would be. Are you rebellious, resentful, all that sort of thing?"

"I don't know," Jennifer said slowly. For the first time it occurred to her that wanting to leave home to experience another kind of life was a kind of rebellion.

"Margo belongs to this club they call La-Clique. I suppose they think that giving it a French name makes it glamorous. Anyway, the kids who belong are not typical of all the young people you'll meet in Hillside or any other place. Sometimes I wish Margo would find other friends, just to have more experience. Not that the girls in LaClique can't be nice enough in their way, but I want to warn you, they're snobbish and they don't let everyone in. I'm not sure whether you'll be invited to join them or not. Oh dear, this is so difficult!"

"Margo told me about LaClique. What is it like, really?"

"For one thing most everyone in it has only one parent and in many cases family difficulties of one kind or another. It's upsetting to some, others take it in stride. As they said in one T.V. show, 'they want it all now.' Good times, that's what it's about. By the way, there's a lot of smoking, lots of drinking; too much, I think. You're going to have to find a graceful way of wiggling out of that, if you want to be sociable and yet hang on to your principles."

"I'll think of something, I hope. Margo seems to be impressed with all her friends."

"Possibly, but she's still dissatisfied. And aimless. I don't know what she's thinking, where she is. After all, I'm only dear old Mums. I hope she'll be decent, but if she isn't, if she gives you a hard time, come and tell me."

Jennifer could not possibly imagine herself complaining about her cousin, but she nodded. Lois continued.

"I think she'll get to love you very much, but she's difficult. As far as the others are concerned, don't forget, there are lots of really fine people there. Don't expect it to be like life in Grant. Now, how about more orange-ade?"

"No, thanks," Jennifer said. As she walked back to the Triumph with her aunt, she realized that life in the suburbs might not be the smooth sailing she had expected.

10.

No place could be more different from the Cowles Ranch than Knolls, the rambling, redwood structure on the side of a hill where Lois parked her car at last.

"It's magnificent! So modern. I love it! It's like a stage set," Jennifer said as Lois unlocked the front door.

"It's humble, but we call it home," she joked and then mused. "Maybe you've struck it right in a way. Stage sets aren't permanent and some of us aren't either."

Jennifer did not quite catch her meaning, but let it go, lost as she was in admiring this place. Unlike the Victorian farmhouse that she knew as home, where rooms were divided by solid walls, here one area seemed to merge with another effortlessly, divided only by an Oriental screen, or a tub of bamboo. Thick, natural-colored rugs, chairs made of curved metal or curved wood that seemed to be molded out of one piece, a long sofa with one arm at the end of it and a wealth of pillows ranging from brilliant roses and pinks to lavenders and blues, an abstract plexiglass sculpture mounted on a stand . . . all this made Jennifer's former ideal in homes, i.e., the Steele interior, dull by contrast.

"Did you decorate this room yourself? It has such spirit."

"A professional decorator helped me, but for the most part the ideas are mine. I'll go over all of it with you sometime, but right now I'm a mess. If you'll pardon me . . ."

For all that Jennifer was impressed with her new home, she could not help but wonder why Margo was not there to greet her. Perhaps she hadn't wanted her cousin to come at all. In that case, Jennifer would not stay too long.

Someone was fumbling with the key at the front door. Margo, she hoped, but instead a pink-faced man, balding, somewhat heavy, but well-tanned, let himself in, stopped in surprise as he saw Jennifer, and then smiled as if he suddenly remembered who she was.

"Let's see, you're the cousin from the Valley, aren't you?"

He had forgotten her name. She helped him quickly. "I'm Jennifer."

"Of course, that's it. And I'm Ted, call me Ted. Lois has been raving about you, how clean-cut and healthy you are. Must be that good country air. Glad you could come and stay with us. Where's Lois?"

"Here I am, dear," Lois said, walking over to peck him on the cheek. A bubble of insight surprised Jennifer: her aunt was acting, pretending to be a loving wife. "We just got home, Ted. Have you eaten? I'm going to make something right away. Poor Jennifer must be starved."

"Not really," she murmured politely.

"Where's Margo? Shouldn't she be here to meet her cousin?" Ted asked.

"She's been at Jody's all day. Jody was having some kind of party, I guess. You know how it is, they forget the time."

Ted frowned. "She should have been here when Jennifer came. Did she make up the bed in her room for Jennifer?"

"No. We decided Jennifer might be happier in a room by herself, so we're giving her the den. You won't mind for a little while, will you?"

Ted frowned and barely murmured he didn't mind, although it was clear this annoyed him. I'm causing trouble, Jennifer was thinking. Margo was hardly eager to see her, and now her uncle couldn't be too pleased about having his den taken over. Maybe Mrs. Cowles had somehow foreseen something like this would happen when she had appeared less than enthusiastic about Jennifer's visit.

"Can I help you get dinner?" Jennifer asked.

"Now if Margo ever offered to do that, I'd keel over," Ted remarked unpleasantly, turning on the huge color television and collapsing on an Eames chair as he snapped open his newspaper.

"I never knew anyone could get dinner so quickly," Jennifer said, trying to be pleasant

78

in the midst of a situation already showing strain. Lois had shoved a frozen dinner into the microwave oven, the coffee was bubbling in an elaborate coffee maker, and the round table with its white formica top in the alcove that made up the dining room was quickly set with place mats.

Will I ever get used to it, Jennifer wondered. Except for the dull buzz and an occasional commercial jingle from the television in the next room, the place was unnaturally quiet and they ate in silence. All the vivacity and charm Lois had displayed when visiting the Cowles subsided, and after a bit Ted took over the conversation.

"Now then, what is it that you raise on your ranch?"

This was followed by a barrage of questions, how much acreage was involved, how many crops, what kind of markets. He appeared genuinely interested in the business end of ranching and seemed notably impressed when, answering his questions about her sheep, she told him frankly the costs involved and the profits she made when she sold an occasional animal at auction or showed them at exhibitions.

Lois, drinking glass after glass of wine and eating little, became more and more withdrawn. Jennifer insisted on doing the dishes and then, as she could think of nothing else to do and thought it impolite to return to the tasteful, but dullish den that would be her room, she joined her aunt and uncle in the living room. Lois, dressed in a long, emerald-green hostess gown, relaxed on the long sofa, while Ted drew the drapes and then stretched out in the Eames chair. The television absorbed them, allowing each of them to sink into a private space of their own making.

Was this what it would be like every night, Jennifer wondered, understanding now why Margo stayed away. Jennifer's hands felt strangely empty. At home they were always busy, with chores or knitting or almost anything at all. Now she fingered the tiny jade lamb that Russell had given her and wondered if her lambs missed her, and if Terry and her mother who had planned to make jam that night were thinking of her, and what Russ was doing that very minute.

"If you don't mind, Lois," she said at last, unable to concentrate for even a minute on the color-saturated eye that took over the living room, "I think I'll take a walk, just to see what it's like around here."

"You won't get lost, will you, dear?" Lois' speech had become slower and the words were slurred ever so slightly.

"I'm used to going out at night. I don't think I'll get lost."

"You can't be too careful around here, and it's getting late," Ted said. "Do you know where you're going to go?" Obviously, he didn't like the idea of her going out alone. But he needn't have worried.

Jennifer opened the front door and was surprised to find herself face to face with her cousin, Margo.

* * *

80

"Margo, am I ever glad to see you!"

Her enthusiasm startled Margo who recovered slowly. "So you finally got here!" She surprised Jennifer by embracing her quickly. Maybe they would be good friends after all. But just as quickly she stepped back and a certain reserve in her eyes puzzled Jennifer.

"Where were you going just now?"

"Out for a walk."

"For a *walk*? Nobody under sixty goes for walks. Everyone jogs. Or bicycles. Or drives. But nobody walks."

She said this with an air of authority that may have been meant to insinuate that only ignorant country cousins wouldn't know that.

"I don't really care about the walk. I'd rather be with you, Margo, whatever you want to do."

"Can't do much now. I'm bushed. Been swimming. Hi, Mom . . . Hi, Uncle Ted!" she called out. *Uncle* Ted? But Jennifer herself would find it hard to call this man Dad under any circumstances. He grunted hello at Margo, but Lois turned her head around.

"Hello, darling. Home now, are you? Come in. I thought you were going to stay at Jody's all night."

"I was, but Jody had a fight with her father. He didn't want her smoking, particularly in the house, and she said everyone did it, and ya-da-da, ya-da-da, so I split."

"Now, Margo, you weren't smoking over there, were you? I told you distinctly that Jody's father can get fairly violent on the subject."

"Mom, I wasn't the only one. Everyone was puffing away. And it could have been lots worse than cigarettes, if you know what I mean. By the way, I'm all out. Can you lend me a few?"

"I wish you wouldn't," Lois said weakly. "You're so young and they aren't kidding when they talk about lung cancer."

"Then why do you do it, Mom? Let's not be such hypocrites. Are they in your drawer?"

"Yes, but take only one. Maybe if we cut down we can break the habit."

Ted turned around to watch Margo as she left the room. "I'll bet they don't do that where you're from."

Jennifer laughed. "I'm afraid it probably happens quite a bit."

"But you don't expect to take up smoking?"

Her apparent virtue would not help her relations with Margo, so she only shook her head no rather quickly.

"C'mon, let's go to my room where we can talk."

"Great!"

Both girls took off their sandals and sat on Margo's bed; now it was intimate and friendly, the way Jennifer had hoped it would be.

"Love your room, Margo. My sister, Terry, would fall in love with it."

"Really? It's okay."

Jennifer would have to write and tell Terry about it: the lacquered white furniture that contrasted with the softer materials of the

82

room, the delicate blues and greens in the rug, the wallpaper and bedspread. A number of dolls and stuffed animals were placed around the room as if Margo were still a child.

"Your house is really beautiful. I've never been in one like this before."

"I suppose. But it gets boring unless you adore television. Do you?"

"No, I hardly ever watch it. Once in a while, maybe. What do you *do* here?"

"What kind of question is that? What do we *do*?"

Jennifer blushed, wishing she could get on the right side of her cousin.

"Do? All right, Jennifer, let's see. H'm. Nothing. That's what we do. On the other hand, we do everything. . . ." She laughed at the contradiction. "I told you about LaClique, didn't I? We have parties: beach parties, pool parties. Sometimes we go into the city. My mother insisted I go to summer school and Ted backs her up. Did we ever have a fight! We compromised. I'm only taking one course. Math. Grrrr."

"It seems odd to think of you studying math. Somehow I think of you doing something more dramatic like dancing or painting."

"I've been through that. My mother ambitiously pushing me to class after class. But I'm not into that anymore. What I really like is the free and easy life. I wish my life could be one long party."

"Really?" Such a thought had never occurred to Jennifer. Her *whole* life? How different she and her cousin were!

"There is going to be one fantastic party a week from Saturday. And at the end of August there's a real party. Ellie Tomlin's father is very conscious about social things, and so each year he puts on a big bash. All the Clique goes to it and lots of others, too. Formal. Almost nobody wears anything like that out here, but they come from the east and so . . . I wonder if you'll still be here then."

"I wonder, too," Jennifer said, wishing her cousin were more eager about her visit. Margo lit another cigarette, blew out the smoke.

"What do you think you'll do with yourself while you're here, Jennifer?"

"I hadn't thought about it much."

"It could be a problem. I spend lots of time with my friends and I'll warn you right now, they like to be exclusive. You might not enjoy them."

"I see." Jennifer was already beginning to feel she wouldn't measure up to the standards of LaClique, whatever those standards might be. "I can take care of myself. I don't want you to feel that you have to do anything for me."

"But I want to, Jennifer. I can introduce you to some of my friends. I just wouldn't want you to feel disappointed if you were left out."

"I'm sure I could cope," Jennifer said.

"Maybe you could be a special member, just for the summer."

Jennifer was tempted to tell her cousin to keep her club, but there was no point getting off on the wrong foot.

"We'd better do something about your clothes before you meet anyone. Those pants . . ." Margo shook her head in disapproval. "Where did you ever find those?"

"Mail order. Sears or Wards, I forget. But they weren't cheap." In fact, Mrs. Cowles had sighed at the way prices were going up when she ordered them, but insisted on getting "best" of the "good, better, or best" categories.

"They don't fit you, Jennifer. They're a mile too big and they're not cut right. You've got such a cute figure, Jen, and the purpose of pants is to show it off, not hide it. Like these."

She stood up and turned around, while Jennifer admitted that the way the pants hugged Margo's delicate frame and seemed to lengthen her legs was far more flattering than the "best" pants she was wearing. Margo knew about clothes. For the first time since she knew her, Jennifer thought that here is something positive in Margo, something she knew as surely as Jennifer herself knew about her animals.

"Margo, Lois said something about all of us going to San Francisco together, because I've never been there. I'd like to buy a pair of pants there. Would you help me pick out some with the right fit?"

"You really want *me* to help *you*? I thought you knew everything."

"Good heavens, no! We do our sewing stint in 4-H, but you really know about fashion."

"Sure, I'll help you, if you really want me to," Margo said, still doubtful, but pleased. I'll bet, Jennifer thought, that she's always being told how pretty she is but nobody ever gives her credit for having a brain.

"It's getting cold," Margo said, shivering slightly and wrapping a blue velour bathrobe around herself; it was too large, making her appear more fragile than ever. The conversation came to a halt. Jennifer picked up a photograph in a ceramic, heart-shaped frame on the table next to Margo's bed.

"Who is this handsome man?" she asked, impressed by the self-confidence that somehow communicated itself in the direct blue eyes, and the studied carelessness of the light brown hair. The grin hinted that here was good company.

"Gary Wilson. And 'handsome' doesn't do him justice. He's fabulous. I didn't think they made men like that."

"You told me about him before. Are you in love?"

"I'm not sure. Could be. Actually I haven't known him long because I haven't been here more than a few months. Besides, he just graduated from high school and I have another year to go. But I think perhaps he really does like me. It's funny, he always treats me very gently, as if I were about to break."

"You do seem fragile. Some men like that."

"The trouble is that he's so popular. He's probably spoiled. Everyone is crazy about him. He's got this way of making every girl think she's his girl friend, without saying so in so many words. Right now he's off mountain climbing somewhere in Canada with some students from Berkeley. He teaches tennis, but will only play with the best players. He's a fabulous swimmer. And he's brilliant, too."

"Wow! All that. How did you meet him?"

"He's part of LaClique, although I guess he'll be going off to school soon and that will be the end."

"Maybe not. Maybe he's in love with you, Margo. Does he talk about it?" In other words, Jennifer was wondering if he was like Russell in that respect.

Margo frowned. "He's not shy, but maybe he's careful. I think we were on the verge of a real relationship and then someone invited him to go mountain climbing and he couldn't resist. But he'll be home next weekend. I can't wait. There'll be a party for him; what a party! It will be *neat*."

She picked up the photograph of Gary and pressed her lips to the cool glass that covered it, something Terry might have done. Silence filled the room and a certain closeness. Perhaps it was a kind of emotional turmoil she was picking up in Margo. Possibly it was the smoke. Whatever it might be, she had a sudden need to get out.

"Margo, want to go jogging?"

There, she'd learned her lesson and would not mention walking.

"Oh, I don't know," Margo said, pouting.

"It makes you feel great," Jennifer coaxed her.

"Okay. You talked me into it. I could lose a little weight off here and there," Margo said, although there could not have been the least hint of fat anywhere on her fleshless body. "I detest fat, more than anything in the world. C'mon, let's go."

"We're going jogging," she called to Lois and Ted, and Jennifer waved as she and Margo ran down the stairs, across the grassy lawn of Knolls, and up a curving drive. They stopped at the top of a hill to catch their breath. The glow of the San Francisco lights could be seen as it lit up the sky in the distance.

"Margo, it's so exciting for me to be here. It's like a foreign country, it's so different from home. Thanks so much for inviting me."

"But I didn't invite you. My mother did," she said pointedly.

Knowing that Jennifer was hard put to answer that, she added more kindly, "But I'm glad you're here. There's only one thing . . ."

"What's that?"

"I don't know. I'm a little afraid of you and I can't imagine why. Oh well, let's skip it. I'm getting cold standing here. If we keep on this road it will go in a circle and it will take about twenty minutes for us to get back home."

So, puzzled by her cousin who couldn't seem to make up her mind about her, Jennifer ran with her down the other side of the hill on the big loop toward Knolls.

11.

Five days of her visit had passed and on the early morning of the sixth, Jennifer sat in her room, biting the end of her pen as she began her first letter home. She had already telephoned, tears of homesickness starting in her eyes as she heard the familiar voices, but fortunately Lois wanted to talk with her sister, which saved her from blurting out that she would not mind going back to the ranch earlier than expected.

But what could she possibly write? She stared at the square of pink stationery decorated with a sentimental drawing of two kittens in the corner, Bruce's parting gift, and came to the conclusion that she must sound enthusiastic. After all, her parents had been generous in letting her go, for her help was needed on the ranch.

> Dear Mom and Dad, Kenny, Terry, and Bruce:
> This place is nothing like home. It's a different world.
>
> Lois and Ted's condominium is heavenly, luxurious, modern, like something you see in a slick maga-

zine. Lois says that as soon as you can find time, you must come and visit.

We go to bed at midnight, and I have a hard time not yawning after ten-thirty, but we can sleep as late as we want to every morning. Do you know how I looked forward to this? I thought it would be GREAT, but there I am waking up at five-thirty every day and nobody else gets up for hours and hours. Sometimes I go jogging.

Yesterday, Lois, Margo, and I drove into San Francisco. It's a fantastic place. Margo turned her nose up and said we were doing all the dumb touristy things, like riding on the Cable Car, eating at the Fishermen's Wharf, and going through Chinatown. It was all very beautiful. Then we stopped at a boutique that Terry would have *loved* and Margo helped me pick out some French blue jeans. With a fancy label, whirls of white stitching! Hope my lambs will appreciate it when I get back.

Jennifer paused. There had been so many shops and at last they went to what Margo had said was her favorite boutique, an exciting place with posters and paintings all over, racks and displays of brilliant clothes, suggesting days on the beach, dancing at nightclubs, such as could not be found miles from Freeville. All the while, rock music pulsated through the store. Margo had said she would take her cousin in hand, and so she did, gathering armfuls of clothes and insisting that she try them on. Lois and Margo had passed judgment on them, clucking, approving, or thoroughly disapproving of the various garments. In the end, they agreed that the first thing Jennifer must have were proper jeans and indeed she found herself delighted with the French pair with the famous label, which Margo had suggested. Yet the price made Jennifer blanch. Lois and Margo had applauded when she'd said, of course, she would take them. But it would be best not to go into this detail with her family. She continued.

> Hillside is a pleasant place, a few old homes, many news ones, and a downtown with restaurants and shops with quaint names like Bozo's Bones (a pet store), Sugar 'n' Spice (a boutique), and Hair We Are (a beauty parlor). Margo's high school is much larger and more elegant than Freeville High; it doesn't even look like a school, all glass and wood, rugs on the classroom floors!

> I miss all of you and all my darling animals. Please kiss every one of them for me. The only animal here is a big old Persian cat named Pouf who is very beautiful, but snobbish. She can't be bothered playing with string or catnip mice.

> Please write to me and let me know how everything is. That's all for now.

Love,
Jennifer

There, that did it! She read over the letter, crossed out a few words, and put it in an envelope. The sun was shining over the hills that were still dewy in the early morning. Soon they would take on the heat of the day, becoming dry. Blue mountains in the distance. Lois had promised they would explore it one day and yet. . . .

Her aunt, the vivacious theatrical Lois who had so charmed everyone at the ranch, now showed an aspect one would never have guessed. Lois, dressed as though she had just posed for a photograph in *Vogue*, might cry out good-bye gaily as she left the house for an appointment with her shrink, or a yoga class, or luncheon with a friend, or a tennis game (for her instructor would be upset if he came home and found she hadn't practiced). At such times she sparkled. But at other times she appeared to withdraw, becoming quiet, as if a space around her were meant to keep everyone out. Usually in the afternoons, she would stay in her spacious bedroom, a room such as Jennifer had never seen, painted and colored in everything from pink to a deep rose. One afternoon Jennifer had knocked on the door and brought in her mail, only to find her aunt dressed in a lacy, satin housecoat, such as one imagines movie stars wearing. A novel, a bottle of wine and a wine glass on the table beside her completed the picture, but she was resting on the chaise lounge, her half-closed eyes focused on the view outside the window. She managed to turn toward her niece, moving slowly like a mechanical toy that had nearly broken down, and Jennifer withdrew, worried, knowing something was wrong with her aunt. Was it drinking or something else?

In any event, it was not what she would write home about.

Nor would she mention that Margo puzzled her. At times she acted like a best friend, twining her slender arms around Jen's neck, pulling her into her bedroom so they could talk, or taking her to Hillside's center so they could visit what boutiques there were, always encouraging Jennifer to try this shirt or that bathing suit, judging her. "Yeah. Terrific!" or "Not you. Take it off, quick!" It bothered Jennifer who couldn't well afford to buy anything more, but Margo convinced her that didn't matter in the least. Then they would get into the red Triumph and spin around town before driving straight home, as Lois had ordered. At such times she was like a sister to Jennifer. And then, without a moment's warning, a coldness would creep into her voice and manners, and though Jennifer might ask her to tell her what was the matter, Margo would only toss her head and look away.

She understood none of this. Suddenly she longed for Russell. He would understand. Of course, she couldn't write this to him any more than she would tell her family.

But what could she say? She had already written him four letters and torn them up. Either they betrayed her feelings too strongly, letting him know how much she missed him, or they turned out to be too cold and distant.

Talking was so easy, writing so difficult. If she were home, she would hop on her bicycle, ride over to his place, help him in the barn, for he would be working there at this time; then he would take out a few minutes and they would sit on the rail fence and talk. But now it was time to write as she had promised.

She ran downstairs, breathed in the crisp morning air, and began to jog, hoping the right words would come to her. She must let him think she was having a good time though it would have to be an exaggeration.

She wondered if he missed her. Would he call the other girls in the Club: Susan or Brenda or Connie? She suspected they might be flattered to be invited to meetings or out bowling or to some of the square dances. She must write to him then that morning.

But still it was difficult to write. She could not let him see how homesick she was when she thought of her sweet lambs coming to greet her, all clamoring for attention, or how she used to experience that certain excitement when he called to ask her if she'd like to go riding with him or drive with him to Knight's Landing to deliver a calf to someone there. She thought of the two of them, taking off for a square dance at the Grange Hall. How good it all seemed! How much more exciting than this rather dull existence in which she felt herself more an outsider than anything else.

But she must not let Russ know this. Her letter must sound as if it were simply dashed off because she was too busy to write. Then as she gazed out of the window the problem was solved. She drew a pen line drawing of the hills and the way the Knolls nested against a background of lawn and trees while other hills rose and descended in the distance. She feared she was no better at drawing than writing, but at least the picture gave an idea of the way the land lay.

At the bottom of the page she scribbled:

> Dear Russ:
> It's beautiful here and it's different from home, but it would be much better if you were here. Here's a confession: I miss it all. Everything at home seems great.
> But I'm not ready to come back. Not yet. Please write to me, won't you? My love to your parents and all the kids in 4-H.
> Love,
> Jennifer

As she sealed the letter she heard voices from the next room, a low mumble, a few words practically hissed. "You should . . ." "But you exaggerate, Ted!" Another rumble. Uncle Ted and Lois arguing? The more they fought the lower their voices grew, becoming fierce whispers. Ted appeared to be attacking Lois, who insisted on defending herself in whatever argument went on.

Jennifer shuddered. The quarrel stabbed the freshness of the morning. Quietly, she took her letters and left the house, walked to the mailbox, and dropped them in, then sighed with relief. Once more she had connected herself with home.

12.

On the very day that Jennifer mailed her first letters home, it might be said that her social career was launched. It was a complete surprise since the day had held as little promise as most of the others.

As usual Margo had stayed in bed until quarter to eleven, had then rushed and refused to eat breakfast, a now familiar, furious battle between her and her mother. Then she had fled to her math class.

Lois sighed. "I suppose I should be grateful she's even going. I hope she won't flunk again. Of course, it wouldn't matter to her."

"Maybe I could help. Not that I'm so good, but I managed to get through it all right."

"You are a darling, Jen, but I wouldn't suggest that you offer to help. Margo's touchy. If *she* asks you, that's a different matter."

When Margo failed to return from class, Lois made a shrimp salad while Jennifer took care of the iced tea and they sat together on the tiny patio. It was one of Lois' better days, for although Margo upset her, she was neither falsely cheerful, nor did she seem withdrawn.

"By the way, has Margo talked with you about Gary Wilson?"

"A little."

"Only a little? I ought to warn you about Gary."

"Warn me?"

"He's spectacular, just as Margo says. Charming, a natural winner, superb sportsman, all that. In fact, he's my tennis pro and I couldn't ask for anyone better. But you'll want to be careful. Gary feeds on the adoration of females, no matter what the age is. Resisting him is like turning down Robert Redford."

"You don't have to worry about me, Lois. I'm such a country mouse he won't even notice me."

"Wait a minute. What's all this 'country mouse' business? Margo, I'll bet. Has she suggested something like that?"

"Oh, no, Lois, she never said anything like that. Really."

"Jennifer, there won't be a girl in this town . . . well in that Clique, which isn't saying much, who won't be jealous of you."

"Lois, that's ridiculous."

And yet she knew that in Freeville, girls at school had often been jealous of her, because she was on the gymnast team, because she was class president, because she did spectacularly in 4-H, because Russell was thought to be her boyfriend, any number of reasons. But it couldn't possibly happen here, particularly when her cousin, Margo, was a real beauty.

Lois retired to her room and Jennifer,

yawning, picked up a novel Lois had let her borrow. She would have liked to go swimming in the pool downstairs or to have borrowed her aunt's bicycle and taken a long ride, but she had to wait for Margo. Time meant so little here; at home in summer one could not afford to waste a minute.

"Hey, bookworm, I've got news for you."

Margo, returning nearly two hours after she had left, stood in the doorway. "Two of the girls have decided to meet you."

"I hope it didn't take hours to sweat out the decision," Jennifer said with a sarcasm that was hardly her style. Margo hardly noticed.

"They're curious, you know. Want to see what my cousin is like, and I want to show you off."

"Show me off! But, Margo . . ."

They were to meet about three-thirty at Lukke's, a coffeehouse in the center of town, so there was time for a swim downstairs, time to stretch out on a towel and deepen their sun tans.

"I love being lazy," Jennifer murmured.

"You sound almost human," Margo answered. But the next minute Jennifer glanced at her watch. Wasn't it time to leave? Margo, unimpressed, didn't budge.

"Rule One. Never arrive on time. The trick is to see if you can make the other person wait for you, but you have to time it so you get there just when they're ready to split."

"I see," Jennifer said, thinking how ridiculous this was. Again she was aware that time had no importance to Margo, but she was the guest so she let Margo make the move.

At last they showered and Margo, dressed in bright yellow shorts that showed off her long, slim legs and a sheer, enormous over-shirt that emphasized her slenderness, faced Jennifer as she appeared in her new jeans and a white shirt.

"Don't you know anything, Jennifer? Here, let me fix it!" Margo unfastened the top buttons of her cousin's shirt and tied the tails in front so that a portion of tanned skin showed between shirt and pants. Margo had a touch that made a difference.

Lukke's, once a tiny lunchroom, was extended on a wooden deck, covered with small, round tables and old-fashioned ice-cream-parlor chairs with twisted wire backs. Margo led Jennifer to a table on the side where two girls, both in sundresses that showed off their carefully acquired summer tans, smoked and sipped tall, cool drinks. What was it about them, Jen wondered, that made them so different from the girls she knew?

"Have you been waiting long?" Margo asked innocently.

"No, we just got here," one of them said. "Is this Jennifer?"

"Yes, I'm Jennifer. Hello!"

"This is Cindi Taylor," Margo said of the pretty, round-faced girl whose hair was a cap of short, blonde curls.

"And this is Marcia Ewing." This was the tall, slender, olive-skinned girl whose black hair was pulled to the top of her head and secured there with a rose.

"I'm so glad to see you. Margo's told us so much about you."

"Yes, Margo, why'd you wait so long to introduce us?"

The questions needed no answer. Perhaps the difference between them and the girls Jennifer knew lay in a certain coolness, cool in the sense that they were undoubtedly familiar with every nuance of their particular society, were most likely acquainted with all the latest dances, records, movies, and so on. Those things about which Jennifer knew relatively little. In Grant, they took on little importance. The girls were cool in another sense, too; their feelings were well-controlled. Their words were superficially cordial but they were not in a hurry to overwhelm Jennifer with offers of friendship. On the other hand, Jennifer simply accepted people when she met them.

"Where are you from, Central Valley somewhere?"

"Yes, a tiny place called Grant, north of Sacramento. We go to school in the next town, which is Freeville. It's not famous for anything."

"I've never heard of it. Have you, Marcia?"

"No, only when Margo talked about it."

Jennifer felt them staring at her as though she had just come from Mars.

"I've never even been to the Central Valley. We only pass through on our way to the Sierras when we go skiing."

"I go skiing up there, too," Jennifer said. "At least twice a year."

She had scored with that. They approved. A boy came over to take their orders, his eyes riveting on Jennifer.

"I'll have a root beer float, please," she said and then realized she had probably dropped back in her scoring as Margo ordered a diet drink. Although Jennifer was slender, she felt herself elephantine for having ordered a sweet drink with ice cream, while they, pencil thin, sipped Tab.

"Jennifer, what do you think of Hillside?"

"It's very nice. That is, I haven't seen much yet, but it's very lovely here."

"The truth is she's homesick for her cow," Margo said, an unexpected blow from her cousin who intended apparently to have her appear countrified.

"Do you really have a cow?" Cindi asked.

"Of course she has. You should see her milk her. Swish, swish! Jennifer is very good, wins prizes in milking contests."

"That's not true, Margo. I have nothing to do with that. We have one family cow. We're not a dairy."

"But you do have a lot of sheep. And she's got a cute little lamb that follows her everywhere. And she makes pots of money at the State Fair."

"What fun!" Cindi exclaimed, and Marcia smiled in what Jennifer interpreted as clear condescension. Margo had made her point.

"It's not quite like that," Jennifer said coolly. "My sheep don't make very much

101

money for me now, but I am building up a good flock. The little lamb that follows me around is a bummer, that is, her mother died so I had to raise her personally for a while."

She wished they would stop talking about the ranch since it was clear they had no understanding of what it was really like, that it was a way of life. She turned the conversation back to them.

"Do you all go to school in Hillside?"

It turned out that Marcia went to a private school in San Francisco and Cindi went to a Catholic academy. Margo was new in the community. Was this what brought them together, that in a sense they were outsiders? Or was there something more?

"Tell me, what do you do for excitement in Freeville?" Marcia asked with apparent innocence, but Jennifer wondered if she thought life there would resemble the "Hee-Haw" show.

"We do what people do anywhere, I guess. Parties, square dances; sometimes we go to Sacramento to hear a good rock concert. 4-H has a summer camp. Sometimes we're invited for weekends at the University. What do you do?"

They giggled as though this were a very funny question. Jennifer sat erectly, wondering why they so wanted to put her down.

"We have parties," Cindi said, "sometimes beach parties, pool parties, we go sailing, riding, water skiing, you know. Sometimes we try to get into night clubs in San Francisco."

"And rock concerts there and in Oakland," Margo added.

"My father always gives me a great time when I go to see him. It's always dinner, and then we go to a game or a musical comedy," Marcia said.

"Wish my father would do that, but he's in San Diego, so I don't get to see him any more. What a drag!"

"Jennifer's family is pure. Mama and Papa, two boys and two girls. Just like a nice family T.V. program," Margo said. Perhaps this time she had gone too far, for Cindi and Marcia appeared genuinely impressed.

"That's terrific," Cindi said, her sincerity evident.

"It's amazing. And great," Marcia said. "I just couldn't imagine what it would be like."

Margo shifted the conversation. "Anyone heard from Gary?"

"No, not a word, but I can't wait to see him again. He'll be at the party; that's all I know," Marcia said.

"Wait till you see him, Jennifer," Cindi said. "The boys in LaClique are very cute for the most part, but nobody can begin to touch Gary."

"You can't compare Gary to anyone because he's incomparable. It's an experience just to know him," Margo said.

Marcia smiled at Margo. "She has it bad, but it's true, Gary is fantastic. When you see him, Jennifer, you'll flip."

"I don't think she will," Margo said almost too intensely. "Jennifer has a boyfriend back

103

home. She has this large photograph of him in her room, black wavy hair, a real western type with eyes that look at you clear and direct. He could go into the movies any time."

Jennifer found herself reddening. "He'd be terrible in the movies. He's a rancher and probably always will be. Anyway, he's just a friend."

"Then why the enormous photograph?"

The girls leaned forward, smiling at her, lightly teasing as though Jennifer were a shy child, denying she had a boyfriend. Possibly they were relieved that here was not still another girl in competition for Gary.

"You're blushing!" Cindi said. "Come, tell us the truth."

"You mustn't be shy," Marcia said. "In our group we have this rule. You say what you want to say because if you hold back your true emotions, they get all wormy inside of you."

"Wormy?" Jennifer asked.

"That's what Olga, my shrink, says, too. 'Let it all out, honey.' "

"Cindi, you're not supposed to talk about what goes on in your sessions, but Charlie says the same thing. I go to Charlie," Marcia said.

"Does everyone here go to a therapist or someone? Is that the thing to do?"

Cindi laughed. "You've got it, man. I know at least ten kids and if I concentrated I could think of more. Even then I'd be leaving some out."

"But why is it necessary?"

"Are you kidding? It helps you to cope."

"What's there to cope about?" Possibly she shouldn't have asked. It must have sounded naive. She had problems, but she hadn't had to go to anyone about them.

"There's lots of things to cope with," Marcia said slowly and solemnly. "We're not always able to figure it out by ourselves."

"Well, how would Jennifer know?" Margo said. "She's living in a different century."

Jennifer was suddenly aware of the more important differences in their lives. If they moved around as much as Margo, changing fathers or mothers, it couldn't be an easy life. As for herself, she couldn't imagine her father and mother separating.

"I'm sorry if I said anything that rubbed you the wrong way or hurt your feelings. I didn't know," she said simply and directly.

"It's okay. Don't worry about it," Marcia said. "Different lifestyle."

"How long will you be staying?" Cindi asked. Margo averted her eyes.

"I really don't know. For a little while, I guess," Jennifer said.

"Maybe we'll see you at Gary's party then," Marcia said.

Maybe! A silence followed as though it were an unsettled matter. It seemed as if the most popular girl of Freeville High had just flunked out socially in Hillside and would never make the exclusive LaClique. So, that's how it is! Jennifer thought philosophically.

As she rode home with Margo in the red Triumph, she said, "Your friends are interesting."

"They were ribbing you, putting you on. Couldn't you tell?"

"Of course. But I rather liked them."

"Jennifer, you will never get anything through that head of yours!"

The rooms of the condominium were leaden in their silence as the sun beat through with its late afternoon glare. The door to Lois' room was uncompromisingly shut. Margo lit a cigarette and leaned back against the cushions, as if she too had withdrawn to a private world.

Never had Jennifer felt more out of place. But the mistake could be remedied. She would last through the next week and then find the bus that would take her to Freeville. Maybe Russell would meet her at the bus station!

13.

"Well, you passed," Margo said.

"Terrific! I didn't know I'd been taking any exams," Jennifer said.

It was four o'clock in the afternoon of the day following the meeting at Lukke's, a long, lonely day for Jennifer. Lois had gone to a yoga class, a swimming group, and a meeting of the Gourmet Club. People here seemed to have a passion for improving themselves. But when Lois returned, she hugged Jennifer quickly and went to her room, closing the door behind her.

Margo, dressing minutes before her class was to begin, yelled out she had a dental appointment in the afternoon, but would be home sometime.

Jennifer, alone, took a long walk and blessed the fact that at least she'd have time to take pictures. She passed a girl she would have liked knowing, a tall girl with dark braids who carried a portfolio under her arms. Was she an artist? At any rate, she was friendly and most likely not a member of LaClique. How could she tell? She wasn't sure. But she had come across several people she thought she would like knowing, but when she had asked Margo about them, she had simply shrugged them off.

Jennifer took a swim, and then picked up the sweater she was crocheting. It was four when Margo breezed in with the news that Jennifer had "passed."

"LaClique, of course, dummy. Frankly, I don't know why Cindi and Marcia think you'd fit in with the rest of us."

"You mean I'm invited to be part of it?"

"Not as a member, only a guest. Get that straight. I can't say they were one hundred percent enthusiastic about you."

"If it's so hard for them to decide, they don't have to worry. I'm not one to crash. I don't have to be part of it."

"Come off it, Jen. Sure they want you. The trouble is this: You can't possibly understand us."

"How do you know I can't? Just because my parents are still married? They are so busy trying to keep us alive and together, there isn't time to think about separating, even if they wanted to, which they don't. Am I different because I don't go to a shrink? Or because I happen to know how to milk a cow?"

"All right. All that does make you different, doesn't it?"

"If you don't want me to join, I won't."

"It's not that."

"I don't have to go to Gary's party. I don't mind staying home if it upsets you."

At that Margo turned her head away and did not answer.

"I just want to know one thing, Margo. Why are Cindi and Marcia so hesitant? I want to know what's really wrong."

Margo turned to her, eyes blazing.

"All right then. If you can't see it yourself, I'll tell you. You're unbelievable, like you came out of the Waltons or some other drippy T.V. show. You know the theme: times can be hard, but we all pull together. Mom and Dad are welded together forever and forever. You might have a tiny spat in your family now and then, but never a real breakup. You don't smoke, you don't drink, or do anything else except go to your pajama parties with a bunch of 4-H girls. I can just see all of you giggling and giggling. And drinking milk."

"What's wrong with drinking milk? What does that have to do with it?" Jennifer asked.

Margo shuddered and rolled her eyes.

"Listen, Margo, maybe it would be best if I went home. It's just not working out."

Margo's expression changed abruptly. "You can't mean it, Jen. You wouldn't really go home, would you?"

"Sure, if I'm such a museum piece."

"But you haven't been here long at all. There's so much we haven't done. Forget what I said just now, okay? Of course I want you to join LaClique for the summer and go to the party on Saturday night. We can do all kinds of things together. Please, Jen."

Suddenly the air became stifling, the walls too close. Margo was *pleading* with Jennifer to stay. Maybe lonely people were like that, abusive one minute and loving the next.

"It will be fun. You'll see, Jen. It's been quiet so far, but it will get better. So help me, it will."

"It's too much for me," Jennifer cried. "C'mon, shall we go jogging?"

"If you like, of course," Margo said. "Let me just change my shoes and I'll be with you."

Jennifer waited and wondered if she would ever understand her cousin. At first she didn't want her to go to the dance and would have preferred that LaClique would not accept her; that was clear. But when Jennifer threatened to leave, it changed suddenly, unexpectedly. So she was afraid of her and at the same time she needed her country cousin.

It was all very puzzling.

14.

Nothing seemed to happen and then, on the day of the party for Gary, Jennifer was taken aback with surprise not once but twice.

The first came during the afternoon when Margo glided into the house. "I've got something for you, something you are *dying* to get. But you've got to guess what!"

Margo's eyes were sparkling. Tonight Gary would be back! All day she had played her latest records, humming to herself and dancing around. Now she was teasing Jennifer, not allowing her to see what she held behind her back until Jennifer chased her and they fell over the cushions in the living room, laughing.

Jennifer blushed. A letter from Russell! He must have written it the minute he had received her letter. She began to open it, but on looking up saw that Lois and Margo were watching her, their lips curled in amusement.

"See you later," she said, escaping to her room to read the letter without her aunt and cousin teasing. Although Russell had sent her postcards when traveling, this was the first letter he had ever written to her. His handwriting, strong and decisive, suddenly seemed precious to her. So like him, she thought. She imagined him writing, sitting at his desk.

Dear Jennifer:
Thanks for the sketch. Hope you're having a good time.

Yesterday I went to the ranch to visit your family and spend time with Bruce. He's taking good care of your flock. The sheep look great. He's learning. He noticed that Bo Derek, the Hampshire, seemed peaky. We isolated her for a few days and she seemed so much herself after a while we didn't have to call a vet.

I took the liberty of filling out applications forms for you for the County and State Fairs. By the time they come around you may be ready to come home and show your favorites. Bruce is a good substitute, but I think your little friends are baa-ing for you.

All the 4-H kids say hello and hope you'll write. I too would like to hear all about the wonders of the Bay Area and the suburban life (if there are any!).

Take care,
Russell

Jennifer read the letter over and over. He hadn't signed it with the expected "Love, Russ." Either he was shy or he didn't want to raise her hopes. She tried to read between the lines for hidden meanings, but found none. Still, he had gone out of his way to check on her sheep, to talk with Bruce, and to send for application forms for her at the Fairs.

He must have answered her letter immediately. Did he love her? Did he miss her as much as she missed him? She slipped the letter inside her small diary and went back to join Lois and Margo, who kidded her gently and begged to see the letter, although they knew Jennifer would never show it.

"I think that you are very much in love with Russell," Margo said, "and I'm very glad and relieved."

"Relieved? Why should you be relieved?" Jennifer asked.

Margo stopped short as if she were about to say something, but thought better of it. "I dunno. I'm just glad you and he are in love."

"Wait a minute. That's an awfully strong word. We're friends, that's about it." By all means she must protect herself against illusions. Maybe that's all they were, good friends. She dared not hope for more.

Excitement mounted as the Saturday night party grew closer to reality. As yet nobody had seen Gary, but someone had phoned him and he promised to be at the party. The phone rang all day long, and Margo was giddy with anticipation.

"I can't stand it. I can't eat a thing. My stomach is full of drunken butterflies," she said.

I wonder why it doesn't happen to me that way when I'm about to see Russell, Jennifer wrote in her diary. *If that's what being in love is, I'd like to experience it. But I never seem to lose my appetite.*

"Parties begin late here, don't they?" Jennifer found nine o'clock a strange hour, but when Margo told her they mustn't arrive before nine-thirty at the earliest, she accepted it as that different lifestyle that Lois talked about so much.

She dressed in the formal pink gown she had made for the Spring Prom, and went to ask Lois to help with the zipper.

"But you can't wear that!" Margo cried. "It's much too formal. Nobody ever dresses like that around here. This is a barbecue, a swim party."

Margo herself wore full, silky, white pants and a sheer top, on which a rainbow had been painted. It made her seem an exotic, diaphanous butterfly.

"I guess I could wear my jeans," Jennifer said, although she had worn little else since she'd been there.

"I've got something you can wear, Jen. I haven't even worn it myself, so nobody will know where it comes from," Lois said.

She went to her room and returned with pants the color of a camellia and a georgette shirt.

"Mom!" Margo cried. "You've never let me wear it. I've asked you so many times and here you are giving it to Jennifer."

Jennifer stood between the two of them, knowing she must make a decision. She would have loved her aunt's exquisite outfit, but she could not bear the hurt in Margo's voice. If she took advantage of her aunt's offer, here would be one more thing to spoil the new, friendly relationship she was developing with Margo.

"Thanks a lot, Lois, but I couldn't. It's meant for you. But thanks anyway."

"Jennifer, if you don't try something new, you'll never know what it's like. I'd love to see it on you."

"Maybe some other time," she said. "Actually, I just remembered I have a white sundress. It's a little long, but it might be okay."

"Yes, wear it. It's exactly right," Margo said, relieved and possibly amazed at Jennifer's decision not to borrow her mother's outfit. The sundress was simple enough, all right, but unexciting. "I have a blue chiffon scarf I'll let you take and if you'll let me do your makeup for you, you'll be perfect."

Jennifer sat in front of the dressing table mirror, which was surrounded by many light bulbs while Margo expertly painted her face, and then wrapped the scarf around Jennifer's head. Lois watched.

"Margo, if you ever had a gift, it's that. You touch Jennifer and she could pose for a photograph in *Vogue*."

But Margo ignored her mother's compliment, as if she didn't believe it, as if she didn't care.

"Are you going out tonight, Lois?" Jennifer asked her aunt, who had been dressed in one of her "at home" outfits, a floor-length gown.

"No, Ted's away on business this weekend, so" — she hesitated, smiled weakly — "don't you worry about me. I've got a good novel and Pouf to keep me company. You girls had better get going. I think you are both beautiful and I hope you have a marvelous time. Remember me to Gary!"

"Oh, Mo-o-om!" Margo said in disgust, but Lois only smiled.

"Remember, I want to hear all about it, no details spared."

"Mother, we can't tell you *everything*," Margo teased. But she threw her arms around her mother and embraced her. Never had Jennifer seen her cousin so happy, as if she were in love with the whole world.

Lois gave her daughter the keys to the car. She kissed Jennifer and Margo, and watched them from the window.

15.

Margo loved to drive and she drove well although somewhat recklessly that evening as she headed toward the outskirts of Hillside where the houses were half-hidden among acres of natural vegetation, woods, and fields.

"Do I look all right?" Margo asked nervously, as she parked the car and walked with her cousin to the sprawling, redwood house where the Sotherns were giving the party.

"You're superb. How can you doubt it?" Jennifer asked. It was tiring, having to assure her exotic cousin over and over of her genuine beauty. Margo must know how truly exquisite she was. "And I look like the poster of the girl who says 'I drink milk!' " Jennifer thought. She supposed she was good-looking enough, blooming with health. But she would never possess that delicacy that made Margo unique.

"I'll have to write home and describe this place to my mother," she told Margo, as they walked through the front yard that seemed a tamed woodland. "It's like the home of a movie star, only more natural."

"That's how it *seems*. It's exactly what they would want you to think, that it's entirely natural. I happen to know that the Sotherns spent thousands and thousands to some landscape gardener to get this effect."

"They did?" Jennifer asked with only a little surprise, for she was getting used to the fact that life here had practically nothing in common with life in Grant. The people were entirely different, too, she thought, as a tall, wiry woman in a salmon-colored jumpsuit, which plunged into a V so low that it was difficult to keep from staring at it, came to greet the girls.

"Hello, Margo, you gorgeous thing. So glad you could come. And who is this love of a girl with you?"

"My cousin, Jennifer. Mrs. Sothern. Jennifer comes from an enormous ranch in the Valley." Margo spoke with pride, but Jennifer demured politely.

"It's not really 'enormous.' Thanks for inviting me to the party, Mrs. Sothern. Your place is truly beautiful."

"Oh, do you like it? How nice!" Mrs. Sothern answered, bored, as if she'd heard that remark too many times before. "Everyone's in back. You know the way, Margo." So much for them! Mrs. Sothern's head was already turned toward the next car of guests.

Jennifer whispered she would have loved going through the house, but Margo led her through a gate that led to the back of the house, which, of course, was not the utilitarian, kitchen-garden backyard Jennifer was used to, but a luxurious setting that looked like a scene from a movie. A wide patio, a grassy area on which sprawled a great, live oak tree, the swimming pool shimmering and shining in the very last rays of the summer sunset. Someone was already lighting the Japanese lanterns strung between the trees. Rock music permeated the whole yard, and everywhere people clustered, some breaking away to dive into the pool, some huddling to tell jokes with sudden bursts of laughter. Several of LaClique sat quietly smoking and talking.

It was Jennifer's first view of LaClique, although others must have been invited, too. The T.V. drama held the same message she found here, that life was meant to be fun, first of all.

Margo vanished to join some friends on the far side of the pool, so Jennifer found herself alone. She recognized Cindi diving into the pool and coming up, only to cavort like a lithe porpoise. Marcia and Margo, surrounded by a quartet of attentive men, were guffawing at someone's anecdote.

It was strange to be so alone in the middle of all this frivolity, as if the T.V. drama were going on, but she wasn't part of it. A young man in tartan shorts brushed past her, then stopped.

"Barbie, you're here at last! I've been waitin' and waitin' and waitin' . . ." He paused, then peered at Jennifer closely, for he was either near-sighted or drunk. "Barbie? You're not Barbie, are you?" He was crestfallen at the discovery.

"No, I'm sorry."

"I'm sorry. Oh, I'm so sorry. You're prettier than Barbie, but don' tell her. Do I know you? I do, lemme see now, where did we meet?"

He was saved from further brain searching as another guest tapped his shoulder. A nice-looking person, possibly bookish, certainly gentle in his manner.

"Richard, chum, Barbie's waiting for you, over there, by the table under the pines. See?"

Richard begged Jennifer's pardon and toddled away, not quite upright. "He tends to get carried away early in the evening. I don't believe we've met. Alan Dunham."

"Hi! Jennifer. I came with Margo, my cousin."

"So you're the one she told us about! Welcome! How come I haven't seen you around? Here, you don't have a drink. What can I get you?"

He led her to the bar that was set up on the patio and again she suffered the embarrassment of not being a drinker. Lois had taught her that it was all right to order plain soda, but to do so with conviction, as if ordering champagne.

"Some plain soda with a twist of lemon, please."

"What do you want with the soda?" he asked, pointing to the various bottles on the table.

"That's it," she said, smiling so as not to appear too severe.

"If you want to cheat, it's okay."

She laughed, somewhat artificially. "Not now. Maybe another time."

They moved away from the bar and stood talking, drinks in hand. She was finding him very pleasant, as they engaged in intelligent enough chitchat, and they were getting on well enough when someone called. "Hey, Alan, we're gonna have a race. We need you."

He excused himself, promising to see her later. And so she was left alone again, to nurse a glass of soda water and think how strange it was to be so isolated. She was not meant to be the "life of the party"; nobody could call her that; and yet at parties she had always been in the thick of whatever was going on, dancing, game playing, contests . . . whatever.

What's more, Jennifer found herself starving. Margo had turned down Lois' offer of a light supper, insisting that the food at the Sotherns' would be superb, but it was nine-thirty and Jennifer felt that her interior was one vast hollow. She moved to the table where hors d'oeuvres had been set out, and she overheard a conversation.

"Well, is he coming or isn't he?" asked Mrs. Sothern.

"Mom, you know Gary. He likes to make an entrance. He'll be here." That would most likely be Nancy Sothern.

"But everyone's starving. Let's go ahead. Why everyone makes such a fuss over a man, I'll never know. But I have to leave soon and so I'd like to get things underway."

Two girls who had apparently been brought in to help, took away the empty hors d'oeuvre platters and brought out steaming casseroles, platters of Mexican foods, enormous salads in oversized wooden bowls, and baskets of rolls. A huge bowl of flowers graced the center of the table. Candles were lit, secure against the wind in stained-glass candle-holders. They do this with style, like everything else, Jennifer observed.

"Come and get it!"

The last stragglers climbed out of the pool, dried themselves, and drifted along with all the other groups, moving slowly toward the table, taking plates and filling them. The girls took only a bit of this and a taste of that, to preserve their figures, all of which embarrassed the starving Jennifer whose appetite had not decreased. The guests were all around her, and a few said hello, but then moved on. It's as if I weren't really here, Jennifer was thinking. She left the crowd and sat in a wicker chair at the edge of the patio.

A small boy, presumably a Sothern, ran by with a huge ginger cat in his arms. Mrs. Sothern stopped to ask Jennifer if she were having a good time and without waiting for an answer, strolled on. The ginger cat, having escaped the clutches of young Sothern jumped up on Jennifer's lap, to settle there and share her enchiladas. "Hi, pal. Join the crowd!" she said.

Here was a wish granted at last, a fantasy she had once entertained about going to a party where she would remain invisible, watch and hear everything going on, but not be a part of it. It wasn't such a great wish after all. She felt for the jade lamb on the chain that she always wore and found comfort in it. One day she would go home again.

The stereo played on, softer now, background to the hubbub of noise. Gary's name came up again and again, like echoes, first here, then there, all through the yard and everywhere the insistent question repeated itself like a refrain: Where is he?

Jennifer, as the invisible guest at the party, wondered what would happen if the hero did not return. She also wondered if she should go back to the table for seconds, when a great cry went up.

"He's here. Hey, Gary!"

Loud cheering arose as a tall, slender young man stood at the redwood gate that led to the backyard. He paused, waving his hand to everyone, smiling as if nothing pleased him more than to be with all these wonderful people. Here was the hero of LaClique; here was the movie star.

Questions flew through the air. How did it go? When was he going to try Everest? What was at the top of the mountain?

Gary laughed as his blue eyes, deep set in a lean suntanned face, swept over the party, back and forth. Margo had not exaggerated. Here was one of the most charming people Jennifer had ever seen. Who could say what magnetism was? Other men at the party were good-looking, sun-tanned, athletic in many cases, and certainly attractive. Yet

Gary had about him something more, something not readily analyzed. Tall, well-built, he had dressed carefully in a cream-colored western shirt, expensive, off-white pants, and dark leather boots.

Almost immediately Gary was surrounded by half a dozen girls leading him toward the center of the party. A few boys came forward to welcome him with a hearty clap on the back.

And Margo? Thank heavens, Jennifer thought, she had the sense not to crowd around Gary with the other girls, but stood alone, waiting in front of an oleander. Her eyes danced with excitement and Jennifer could almost sense her heart beating as Gary, catching sight of her, left the crowd, walked over to her, bent down, and kissed her. She will either faint or float away, Jennifer whispered to the cat who had staked a claim to remain in her lap forever.

Someone brought him a wicker peacock chair to sit in, so that he took his place there like a king. He was given a drink. Someone heaped a plate of food for him and everyone crowded around him. Margo, having tired of her reserved pose, sat at his feet while others stood around, asking questions. Had climbing the mountain been *such* an extraordinary feat? Apparently it had. Gary, a born storyteller, held the party in his hands.

Russell . . . Jennifer thought of him . . . though handsome in a different way, charming in a more modest fashion, did not share this magnetism, although he was a natural leader. Girls fell in love with him easily, but their crushes faded, for he never promised romance. Jennifer remembered her aunt's words, to beware of Gary's charms, for he could demand anything he wanted and would usually get it. A natural prince.

No need to worry, Jennifer was thinking. I've never been more invisible in my life.

The night was growing dark. The Japanese lanterns swayed on their wires. Torches were lit here and there. The stereo was turned up and people danced. Gary chose Margo, grinning at her as they danced. Lights twinkled, colors changed, the music set the moods, now sultry, now haunting, a fine party. No wonder everyone had looked forward to it.

She stood alone against a background of bushes, and told herself she had learned her lesson well. She was exactly what Margo thought of her: a country cousin. This party was showing it to her more clearly than her cousin could tell her. She would look up bus schedules and return home on Monday.

Hot coffee had been brought out, for the coastal night had turned chilly. Jennifer went to the table, waited her turn, and filled a small mug of coffee, when her arm was jostled and coffee spilled all over her dress.

"Oh, I'm sorry. Did I do that? Here, I hope it won't stain!" It was Gary himself who spoke, as he dipped a napkin into a glass of water and dabbed at the spots.

"Thanks, it could have been much worse," Jennifer said.

"It's such a pretty dress. Not too much

coffee spilled, I hope. Here, let me get you another coffee . . ." and before she could protest, he did so, giving it to her with extreme care. She had to admit her cousin had been right; nothing in the world could have made her turn away from this man.

"Hello, hello. All right now? Who are you anyway? We haven't been properly introduced, have we? Not that anyone ever is around here. Gary Wilson."

As if she didn't know! "I'm Margo's cousin, Jennifer Cowles."

"Jennifer, Jennifer. You look like a Jennifer."

"And what is that supposed to be like?"

"H'mmm. Very good. I'll let you know in time. Why haven't I seen you before?"

"I'm just visiting for the summer, more or less."

"How do you like it so far?"

"I really can't say. I haven't been here long enough to see the marvelous places everyone boasts about. I guess you're a mountain climber. Do you go very often?"

"Every chance I get."

"It must be very exciting and scary. I've seen movies of climbers, swinging out into space miles above nothing at all."

"It's fantastic. As close to flying as you can get. I haven't done the most exciting climbs yet, but I'm working on it."

"What is it about climbing that fascinates you so?"

"The usual answer is you climb because it's there. With me, it's a little different. I

126

have to get to the top. It's an absolute command."

He grinned and yet Jennifer could see he was serious, too. The ultimate in masculinity! That's how Margo had phrased it, an exaggeration Jennifer had found absurd, and yet she found herself wishing he would touch her, would put his arm around her. There was something about him — clean, sunburned, and rugged; open and yet not open. At the same time she was shocked at herself, the independent Jennifer, feeling this way about anyone, but Russell. She forgave herself, insisting it was only curiosity.

"Shall we dance, Jennifer?"

He danced perfectly, with an easy grace. A better dancer than Russell, she thought at first, but amended it, a *different* kind of dancer.

"Jennie, you're superb, do you know that?" he said when the music stopped.

Almost immediately several girls "happened" to be standing near him and at the same time, to Jennifer's surprise, two boys came up to introduce themselves and ask her to dance.

"Where've you been all night? I never saw you," one said.

"Can I dance with you, whoever you are?" another asked, and presently Alan Dunham came up.

The evening had changed completely. She could dance forever, first with one and then another, but it was Gary who came back again and again, and who sought her eyes though he may have been dancing with Margo or someone else. He returned to her after finishing a dance with her cousin.

"Shall we go it again?"

He whispered into her ear as they danced a slow dance.

"I feel there's so much to discover in you, Jennifer. You're different, do you know that?"

"You are, too, Gary."

"Do you play tennis?"

"No. They taught it after school and I always had to catch the school bus, so somehow — I took up gymnastics instead."

"No kidding! Shall we teach you how to play tennis?"

"Sounds great."

"You said you hadn't seen very much around here. I'd like to take you to some places that are spectacular, or very private, or very special. They can't be found in the Central Valley, I assure you."

The music stopped and before Jennifer could answer, Margo interrupted, her voice strained with anger as she faced her cousin. "Jen, we have to go now. Come on."

"You mean it's time already? But we're just getting started," Gary said.

"It's quarter past one and there's a big sailing thing on tomorrow morning and everyone's leaving," Margo said.

"That's right, there is!" Gary said. "Are you going?"

"I'll be going with Alan." Yet she sounded so despondent, it seemed impossible she would have a good time. Jennifer, knowing very well what the trouble was, spoke quietly.

"If you want to go now, Margo, I'm ready. Good night, Gary."

"Oh, you're going?" he asked, disappointment in his voice. As she turned, he pulled her toward him. "You know what? I'm not going to the sailing race and I take it you're not going either. Why don't I show you some of the country? We can ride, hike, anything. Do you have hiking boots or sturdy shoes?"

"Sure."

"I'll be waiting outside your place, at the Knolls at nine. Good night, Jennifer."

He kissed her quickly and then, as Margo waited, he bent over to kiss her, too, in an appeasing way to quiet her, as one calms a child about to have a temper tantrum.

On the way home, Jennifer sat silent, unable to think of a thing to say that would comfort her cousin who shook with anguish.

"That's why I didn't want you to come. That's exactly what I was afraid of, that he would see *you* and want *you*, because you're new and different and gorgeous. Oh, I wish you'd never come at all!"

Jennifer tried to deny that anything had happened and to explain that Gary was only being polite, but Margo would not be comforted. She drove up to Knolls, pulled on the brakes with more force than was necessary, and hurried upstairs to her room, slamming the door behind, leaving Jennifer alone.

16.

Margo, who could scarcely arouse herself before eleven each morning, was, at six, already dressed in a navy blue and white outfit that seemed appropriate for sailing. Jennifer, her face slightly flushed after a restless night filled with dreams involving Gary and mountain tops, admired Margo.

"You look super. You're going with Alan?"

Margo, tight-lipped, made no answer as she brushed her hair.

"He likes you very much, can't keep his eyes off you. I watched him with you last night. He's very nice. Good-looking. I had a chance to talk with him a little."

"You had a chance to talk with everyone 'just a little,' didn't you?" Margo asked, her voice burning with resentment.

"You mean Gary? For heaven's sake, Margo, don't be angry. He spilled coffee over my dress and wanted to make up for it."

"He did a lot of making up, leaving everyone else out."

"It doesn't mean anything. I'm new here and so I'm a novelty, but that's all."

"I don't want to hear another word. Why

don't you go back to Russell? Go back where you belong," Margo said bitterly, slamming the door behind her.

Maybe I will go, Jennifer said to herself, but after today. She wanted to see Gary again, after the strange dreams of the night before.

The doorbell rang and Jennifer let Alan in. Margo scurried out of her room and rushed straight toward Alan, ignoring Jennifer as though she didn't exist. Margo recovered her composure enough to smile up at Alan, as though she could not think of anything more wonderful than spending this glorious day with him.

Jennifer left a note for her aunt on the breakfast table.

Dear Lois:
I don't want to wake you, so I'm writing to let you know I'm going out with a friend and will be back by dinner or else I'll phone.
Love,
Jennifer

Dressed in jeans and shirt with a sweater tied around her shoulders, for the breeze was fresh and she knew it could be foggy and cold along the coast, Jennifer sat on the steps of Knolls and waited for Gary, wondering what kind of car he would drive. She decided it would be anything but an ordinary car, and so was startled to see a huge, black motorcycle zooming up the driveway and stopping short in front of her.

"Gary, it's you! You have a bike?"

"Nope, I just stole it. Here, let me look at you."

She stood up, camera dangling from her shoulder. He came close, his eyes commanding hers to look into his, and then he kissed her. It surprised Jennifer, yet it was ever so pleasant. Possibly it meant little, only another difference between the way one lived here and the way one lived in Grant.

"I've never been on a bike before, and I've always wanted to," she said brightly, although until this moment the thought had never crossed her mind.

Gary handed her a white helmet.

"We have to protect that pretty head of yours. You're valuable, you know."

He placed it on her head, securing it with the chin strap. As his hand brushed across her cheek, she felt a quick whirl of excitement. She was tempted and yet could not possibly tell him that he was ever so handsome in the morning light.

"Have you had breakfast, Jennifer?"

"A glass of milk. That's all."

"On a Sunday morning? We can do better than that. Hop on my putt and let's go!"

I'll remember this day as long as I live, she was thinking, sitting on the black leather seat behind Gary, as she hugged his lithe body, too tightly at first and then more easily, feeling the grace and power in his back as they rode down the road, turned, then roared up the hills westward, leading toward the ocean. They passed fields and groves and pastures where fine horses, such as Mrs. Steele would have adored, grazed. It was incredibly beautiful country with its curves and hills, eucalyptus groves, pines, and bold contemporary houses that nestled in greenery or thrust up from the steep hills, which grew ever steeper and more curved as the Suzuki roared westward. The morning fog had burned off, leaving a sky of bright blue.

If only they could see me now, Jennifer thought. Terry, Bruce, her parents, Russell. . . . Oh, no, what *if* Russ should see her? What would he say? How would he feel? And what about Margo? The red color of guilt tinged the morning momentarily, and then she reasoned that Margo did not *own* Gary. Why, nobody ever really owned anyone. And she was having the most exciting time since she'd come to stay with her cousin.

A heavenly day. This was a fantasy coming true. This was the most exciting man she had ever met. But realistically it would not last. When Margo would find out the country cousin had spent the day with Gary, she would beg and demand that Lois send her home. And Lois would do so, but it mustn't spoil her day.

Gary turned off to a narrow road that led to Muir Woods, a state park. He parked the Suzuki, they got off, he paid entry fees, and they walked together through the woodsy path that led through a grove of giant redwoods.

133

"You've never been here before, Jennie?"

"No. Lois mentioned it but never got around to taking us here."

"Incredible! You spend your life in California and you haven't seen this. Jennie, love, we're going to have to make up for all you haven't seen and done!"

The trees rose silently on both sides of the path, reaching up to the sky, giants so tall that although the sun was shining brightly, it was dark and chilly below on the path. Here and there a ray of sunlight broke through the forest dramatically.

"You won't mind if I take pictures, will you?" Jennifer whispered to Gary, for the whole place had the atmosphere of a cathedral and it was more natural to whisper than to talk out loud. "It won't embarrass you if I do this, will it? Is it awfully touristy?"

"What a ridiculous idea! The trees are honored by your attention. Shoot away."

It took some time for her to adjust the camera, but Gary waited patiently. She took a number of pictures, some aimed straight ahead, others peering upward so that she would get the trees converging high up above the ground.

"And now, Gary. May I take one of you?"

He consented graciously and she took several pictures of him. "Because I'll always want to remember my first day in the redwoods," she explained.

As they walked, he stopped once to explain how the age of a tree could be determined by the rings. He spoke knowledgeably about the animals and birds that lived there and about the way trees sometimes caught fire. He had a good mind, Jennifer was thinking, but what she sensed in him was another facet of his personality, a quality of freedom such as she had never known in anyone else. In a way Russ was free, certainly individual, in his thoughts, and yet Gary was different.

"And now," Gary said as they finished their walk through the woods, "are you starving as much as I?"

"Where can we find something to eat?"

"Leave it to Uncle Gary. I know a fantastic place."

Once more they put on their helmets and mounted what Gary called his black horse and drove north. Jennifer found it frightening, for the road was a ribbon cut into the side of steep embankments, and she dared not look at the sheer drop below. From time to time cars whizzed by with merciless closeness. Scary and yet exciting.

Finally, Gary pulled off to the left, stopping in front of the tiniest lunchroom Jennifer had ever seen, the living room of a shack turned restaurant. The menu written on a blackboard surprised her with its offer of six kinds of coffee, health foods, and sweet rolls with a note that only pure, natural products were used.

They sat at the counter and Gary ordered coffee and snails for them both.

"Snails?" she questioned.

"You don't know 'snails'? My, my! Rolled-up coffee cakes, delicious, with real almond filling. And now, Jen, question time. You have a big ranch, do you, with husky brothers and pretty sisters, and acres and acres?"

"Wait a minute. Be prepared to get disillusioned." She answered his questions briefly. "And now what about you?"

"There's nothing to tell."

"Gary, you know that's not true. Everyone has something, some story."

For a moment he changed, the features resolving into a soberness entirely inconsistent with the sporting lightness she thought characterized him. Here was a secret, but he would not give it to her then.

"My story will have to wait. Such as it is," he said, then snapping back into the lively, on-the-go Gary, he added, "Do you want more breakfast? No? Then we'd better get going. We have a long way ahead of us."

"Where are we going?"

"You'll see."

They drove along curving highways. A flock of sheep in a meadow brought to Jennifer an aching desire to be with them, to hear their bleats, to hold a tiny lamb close to her. But Gary, eyes straight ahead, drove on.

Was it sentimental nonsense that made her catch her breath as they passed still another flock of sheep? Here she was riding on what had to be the most handsome of motorcycles, with her arms clasped around the body of a man who fascinated her as nobody else had ever been able to, and everything in her life promised to bloom, fulfilling a dream. And yet, something in her wanted to

136

go to the pasture to look at the sheep and to sense their mood.

Gary turned to her, then pulled up to a small parking lot by a red barn. They got off the bike and stretched their legs.

"This is Point Reyes," he said. "We're going to hike to the ocean. All right?"

They hiked along the trail, sometimes holding hands and swinging them, sometimes not, as the path sometimes widened and occasionally narrowed. A troop of Boy Scouts, walking single file, passed them, and once Jennifer caught sight of a man and a woman riding two chestnut horses, at which, in spite of her contentment, an ache rose like a lump in her throat as she thought about Russell and herself. But why think of him when she was with Gary?

"Have you always lived in Marin County?" she asked Gary.

"Not always. I've lived here, there, everywhere. Been around."

"Far?"

He shrugged his shoulders as if he didn't want to talk about it, and then changed the subject. "You're a sturdy hiker. Want to go mountain climbing?"

She laughed. "Sure, but I couldn't begin to do what you do. I'd be scared. It's such a risk."

"Yeah, it's dangerous. That's what makes it worthwhile. You have to be alert, sure-footed; you can expect to suffer freezing and muscle cramps. Know how to take care of it. You practice and practice and yet you're always coming up against new situations and you have to guess right, or it may very well be your last guess."

"Doesn't it mean anything to you, taking your life into your hands like that?"

"My life? That's why climbing is so sweet. The mountain challenges you and you dare with the dearest thing you have. And yet, nothing else will purify you so. It's almost like fire."

"Why do you need to be purified?"

Again a shadow passed across Gary's face and then laughing, "You're a funny girl, asking that. Then again, maybe you're so pure you don't need to be purified. Is life all that easy on a ranch?"

"Of course not. It's a gamble, not as dramatic as mountain climbing, but you take chances all the time. You have to plant the right crop in the right field according to what you think the market is going to do. Then it's possible that something happens in Russia or someplace else, the government will step in, and you can't quite cover the loans you had to take to get your crops in. Then you've got the weather. Let it rain at the wrong time and your fruit trees won't be pollinated. A long spell of heat, or a dry year without rain, and it's finis."

"Is it really like that, Jennifer? I'm such an outsider I wouldn't know. I get my ideas from the movies. Horses, range lands, cowboys, pretty girls at home . . . all that."

She laughed and he joined her. "You *are* a dreamer."

138

He wanted to know everything about life in the place where she lived, not with the air of superiority that Cindi and Marcia had shown, but with genuine curiosity. Did most of the friends she had feel they were destined to stay on ranches or obliged to do so? How did they amuse themselves? Were they never curious about what went on outside the farming community? Did they ever have all-night parties, parties without chaperons?

"It's hard to say," she said, answering him as well as she could. "Because not everyone's alike. Isn't that true wherever you go?"

"Of course," he said. There are real differences between the way we take our lives here in Marin and the way you live in the Valley. For myself, I love the feeling of freedom. I could never be tied down, either physically to one place or mentally, either. And do you know something, little Jennifer?"

"I'm not 'little Jennifer.'"

"Forgive me, that was meant to be a pet phrase, not a way of putting you down. I wouldn't think of it because I find you wonderful. What I'd love to do is see you develop, grow, blossom. Learn to be free to live your own life in your own way!"

Before she could answer she caught a glimpse of blue and green between the branches of a tree and heard the roar of waves. "The ocean!" she cried, excited. Gary took her hand and they ran ahead up to a small rise of land. Below them lay the sandy beach and beyond that the Pacific.

"Oh, it's so great! I hadn't imagined!"

White caps moved like points across waves now green, now blue. Waves rolled in, rising proudly to a height and crashing, invading the shore and retreating. A flock of cormorants skimmed over the surface and disappeared from view.

Jennifer and Gary ran down to the beach, took off their shoes and socks, rolled up the legs of their jeans, and walked along the water's edge, letting a wavelet rush in, all lacy white and cold, to wet their feet. Here the sky, no longer pure blue, was whitened with clouds that shut out the sun, so that sometimes Jennifer put on a sweater, and only had to take it off again when the cloud had moved away from the benevolence of the sun. Once, when Jennifer shivered with the cold, Gary put his arms around her, drew her to him, and rubbed his hand along her arm briskly.

"Warmer now?"

"Yes, thanks a lot."

The warming gesture turned into a long embrace and a kiss, his lips tasting the sweetness of hers for a long time. At last he released her.

"Jennifer. Jennie, I've never met any girl like you and I've known a great many girls.

"Be careful." Lois' warning flashed through her head. "And how did you feel about those other girls and how am I so very different?"

They interrupted their talk to watch a dozen sandpipers run up to shore, barely escaping a wavelet, then following it back to see what booty they could catch.

"I like girls. I like their femininity, their

sensitivities. But I also like the strong girls, the ones who'll climb mountains. I think you could do that, Jennifer. I like girls who have good minds. Like you. No matter what they are, though, they want to be loved."

"And men don't want to be loved?"

He grinned. "Sure they do."

"Do you give these girls that love they need so desperately?" She spoke with slight scorn in her voice, for girls who would demean themselves to ask for it so bluntly, like Margo; and yet what was it she was seeking?

"It depends. Look, Jen, you don't expect me to tell tales, do you?"

She wondered, did he really like them all, or did he like to notch them off? This one loves me, that one adores me, and so on.

"You don't approve, do you, Jennifer?"

"Approval isn't the right word. I know what's right for me. But I won't pass judgment on anyone else."

"So tolerant of you!"

"It sounds ugly when you say it like that. As if I felt superior. But I don't, not at all. I want to be loved, too, but it's not the only thing in life." She broke off. "It's hard to put it into words."

"Then don't try. When you're ready, you'll be able to. Possibly you can't put it into words because you're going through a transition. In a way you left the ranch, but you haven't arrived anywhere else yet. You're not really sure how you want to live, are you?"

"Why, Gary! I hadn't thought of it." But

141

he was perceptive, telling her what she feared, that possibly she wanted to change. It was too painful to think of now. He had come too close.

"The sun!"

It had lit up the edges of the huge, puffy clouds and now it emerged, lighting up the skies, the ocean, and the clear profile of Gary beside her. Light played on his hair. Gulls circled above, screaming and mewing. One plunged into the water and rose with a small fish wriggling in his beak.

"It's almost too much, Gary. All this space. All this light. It's almost as if I were flying."

He laughed and hugged her. The wind tugged at their clothes, blew their hair, threatened to blow them away. They climbed rocks, while the surf roared below them. Gary held his hand out to help her up a boulder and together they sat on the high, flat surface, looking out across the water.

It was not so unlike the television drama after all.

Gary kissed her, enchanting her with the sweetness and strength of his embrace. Now she really understood Margo's anguish, as she felt herself irresistibly drawn to this man. And she wondered what would happen next.

Yet only minutes later he frowned at his watch.

"Damn, we have to get back. I've got an appointment at five-thirty and I can't afford to miss it."

They climbed down the rocks, ran back to the beach, and put on their socks and shoes, hiked and jogged back to where the bike was parked, saying little in their haste. They adjusted their helmets, got on the Suzuki, and started back. This time, Jennifer hardly noticed the loveliness of the landscape as she buried her head in Gary's strong back or raised it to feel the wind rushing toward her burning face.

For the first time an unknown agony seared her. What was this important appointment of his? Another girl?

She instantly denied her jealousy. She had no claims on Gary. He could go where he pleased; it was no business of hers. And yet the knowledge hurt, like a pebble in a shoe.

At last he pulled up in front of Knolls.

"Thanks, Gary. It was a fantastic day," she said politely like a well-mannered girl, not someone on the brink of falling in love. She dared not admit to herself the fear that this was the end. She hesitated briefly, then turned to leave when he stopped her.

"Hey, Jennifer, what about tennis?"

"I don't know how to play."

"You already told me. I'll teach you. Meet me Tuesday at seven-thirty, at the courts. Okay?"

"Sure, but I don't have a racquet or balls."

"Not to worry. I have all the stuff you'll need. It's a date then?"

Her face lit up as though she had received a reprieve. She would see him again. Smiling, she waved to him as he started the motorcycle and sped away.

Someone was watching her. She looked up and saw Margo at the window. She had seen it all.

The glow faded as she climbed the stairs and walked into the living room.

"Hello, hello!" she called out as cheerfully as she could.

"Jennifer? I'm glad you're home, dear. We're having some tea. Come join us."

Tea meant a scotch and soda for her aunt and a Coke for Margo. Lois relaxed gracefully on the sofa, but Margo stood by the window tensely as her cousin came in.

"I'd love to join you," Jennifer said, "but believe me, I need a shower first."

"Thanks for the note, dear, but you might have told us where you were going and who you were with," Lois reproved her.

"Right. I went with Gary but I didn't know where we were going. He wanted to show me Muir Woods and Point Reyes. We rode on his bike, walked around a lot, and that's it. Frankly, I'm pooped."

"No wonder," Lois said. "Gary can be formidable. He expects you to be a star athlete like him. If you kept up with him, he's probably impressed."

"I doubt that!" Jennifer said, mostly for Margo's sake. Her green eyes had turned poisonous and Jennifer felt sorry for her, understanding her jealousy. "By the way, Margo, Gary said something nice about you. Let's see . . . that you're extremely beautiful and delicate, something like that."

144

"Thanks so much," Margo said scornfully, but her face seemed to relax at this white lie. Still, she had not, would not, forgive Jennifer.

"What are you girls going to do tonight?" Lois asked languidly.

"I don't know and I don't care what Jennifer is doing, but I'm going to the movies with Alan."

"Terrific. He's so nice," Jennifer said, but Margo turned ray-gun eyes on her.

"I guess I'll stay home and write some letters," Jennifer said.

She had planned to write to Russell, but now hesitated. What could she possibly tell him?

Suddenly her life had became complicated.

Tired enough after the long day's outing, she soon fell asleep, but awoke several times during the night and each time she stared into the dark as she tried to figure out the peculiar dilemma that involved her. She was being torn in so many ways.

Gary was mysterious, daring, filled with a certain vitality and quickness she had never encountered in anyone. Yet she found herself thinking of Russell, too. It would hurt him to know how she felt about Gary. Yet, he had no holds on her. Why, he might be going out with someone back home for all she knew! And yet, she could not stop wondering about him.

And then there was Margo! It would do no good to point out what a nice person Alan was and how he apparently adored her, or to explain there were other things in life, not just boys. Margo was in love with Gary. Her whole being was centered on him. And here was her cousin, Jennifer, dancing with him, spending a whole day with him, allowing him to teach her tennis. Poor Margo!

There was only one thing to do, one decent thing and that would be to thank her aunt and uncle and go home. But she had promised Gary to meet him at the tennis courts. Well then, this would be her last week, her very last week. Margo deserved that at least.

17.

She rose far earlier than was necessary on Tuesday, stretched out lazily in bed, and saw the fog as it brushed against the window. Hillside was becoming beautiful, promising to open like a blossom, fulfilling the promise of the T.V. dream. And all because of Gary.

Nevertheless, she bounced out of bed and tried on the white tennis dress Lois had lent her. She was becoming too generous, pressing clothes, food, and little gifts on her niece. Jennifer had objected as tactfully as she could, because she knew that Margo resented it. Instead of the tennis dress, Jennifer put on her own white shorts, which made her legs appear long and honey-tanned, the sleeveless jersey that served her arms the same way, and the blue band she tied around her head to hold back her hair. Did she look all right? Never in her life had she worried so much about her appearance.

She let herself out of the house quietly, borrowed her aunt's bicycle, and rode over to the tennis courts, almost bumping into Gary on his tenspeed coming from the opposite direction.

"Magic! We meet and we're on time. My God, Jen, how can anyone look so gorgeous this early in the morning?"

147

"Do you say that to everyone?"

"Sure. I'd better if I want to keep my job. But in your case, I really mean it."

"I hope you'll think so when we're finished. Gary, I don't know anything about tennis."

"So much the better. You're unspoiled and you won't have to unlearn bad habits. I've brought you a racquet. Shall we begin?"

Now he became the instructor: cool, direct, firm, throwing his whole concentration on teaching. He helped Jennifer establish various positions, made sure she held the racquet in exactly the right way, that her arms and legs, her head, her spine were working together to bring out the best possible stroke. She had never met anyone so thorough as he explained the fundamentals of the technique and corrected her until she herself could feel the "rightness" of her movements. Then when she understood what he wanted, he would grin. "Hello, hello, hello!" It meant that she was catching on.

"And now, let's try a simple volley on the court and see how it goes."

Her nervousness fled as she found him patient, kind, demanding, and firm. A perfectionist. He would shout a single word of praise when she moved well, even though she might slam the ball into the net. And when she missed, snapping her fingers in self-disgust, he stopped to tell her not to do that; at this point, it didn't matter if she missed. Moving correctly, "flowing," as he called it, was what mattered most now.

When the hour was up and they walked off the court, he glanced at his watch. "You did so well, Jen, I'll treat you to a cup of coffee and then I'll have to rush back."

"Did I really do all right? You're not just saying that?"

He spoke with such seriousness, she blushed at the hint of rebuke in his remarks. "Jennifer, I don't lie, I don't cajole, I don't pretend when I'm teaching. There's no room for petty ego when you confront a challenge. That's the first thing you learn."

As they sat in the booth, she asked him what kind of work he did.

He clapped his hand to his forehead. "What are you doing to my self-confidence? I give you the benefit of my profession and you ask what I do. I'm a tennis coach, love."

"Of course. Forgive me. In that case, I should pay you for lessons. I really want to. Please, let's do it that way."

"Not on your life. I invited you, remember. I've got a vested interest here. I want to train a good partner for myself, someone who will give me a tough time and I think you're the one who can do it."

"I'm afraid I won't be here long enough to get very far. Someone said you only play with pros. Who do you teach?"

"Anyone who asks, unless I find a really hopeless case. I like teaching little kids to start them off correctly. Sometimes I teach their mothers, and sometimes, their grandmothers. I also have a number of businessmen, young executives who want to brush up on the game, and slightly older men. Poor guys, I work them hard."

"But when you play?"

"I'm particular about my partners."

"That's fantastic. All these people want to study with you and you're still going to high school."

"Correction. I'm through with that. Next year college. I'll be living in San Francisco because I've an apartment lined up there, but I'll be going to CAL in Berkeley. I've got lots of ideas about that apartment, about certain people I'd like to have visit me there. Certain beginners in tennis who are promising."

Jennifer, not quite able to handle the implication about visiting Gary in his apartment, smiled her apology.

"You baffle me, do you know that? You have a certain quality that not many people have, and I can't quite figure it out. Now, I've got to split to meet with another woman."

"Oh, ho, making me jealous?"

"Sure. This one is a *grande dame* of eighty-three, but she packs a wallop and demands a lesson three times a week. Do they do that in Grant?"

"No, but I've seen a woman in her nineties running an eighty-acre ranch and making it work. I'm not sure that's easier."

"Touché! I'll call you later, Jen. About tonight."

"I'd love it!"

He paid for the coffees, kissed her, and left. She bicycled home slowly. She ought to write to Russell, but could she do so without mentioning Gary? Without a word about the dreadful strain that had risen between her

150

and Margo? Why did life have to be so complicated!

"Where were you?" Margo demanded as Jennifer let herself in the door.

"Playing tennis. Aren't you up early today?"

"Couldn't sleep. You were playing with Gary, weren't you?"

"He suggested that I learn. There's no reason why you couldn't take lessons, too."

Margo perched on one of the small, white stools her mother kept in the kitchen, one knee pulled up to her chin, the other leg extended. In that position she could have posed for an illustration in a magazine, but the green eyes blazed dangerously.

"If there's anything in my life I'm sorry about, it's the day my mother invited you here. She said, 'Wouldn't I like a companion, someone who'd be like a sister?' The worst part is that I really liked you and wanted you. What an idiot I am! You snatch away the only person I've ever loved."

"Margo, listen. I didn't go after him. He was just being kind, that's all."

"Then why don't you be kind and go home? I need a companion as much as I need a rattlesnake."

"What's going on? Margo, are you being tiresome again?" Lois yawned, as she walked into the kitchen in her dressing gown. "Not another word out of anyone until we have our coffee. Good, black coffee."

Her voice slurred more than usual and as soon as she put up the coffee, moving slowly and uncertainly, she sank into a chair.

151

"Do you want me to get breakfast? I can make something, pancakes, muffins, anything you want," Jennifer said.

"Too fattening," Margo said, plunking down a package of diet crackers on the table. "But that's our good, clean, wholesome, 4-H girl, wanting to show off again."

"Margo, go back to bed and get up on the right side, will you?" Lois asked. "What's the matter with you anyway?"

"Nothing, excepting that our country cousin is getting Gary into her clutches. And I wish *she'd go home!*"

Her voice rose shrilly on this last and she ran into her room, slamming the door. The aroma of fresh coffee filled the tiny kitchen, the sun shone through the window with as much brightness as anyone could ask, and yet Margo had fled to her room, and her aunt, pulling her ice-blue negligee around her, peered into her own private thoughts.

It was all so mixed up. She had never felt so high in her life, practically floating. Yet because of that Margo suffered. And her aunt was faced with still another problem.

Jennifer poured a cup of coffee and gave it to Lois, put up a slice of toast for her, brought down jam from the pantry shelf.

"Come on, Lois. It will make you feel better."

"Jennifer, what am I going to do about Margo?"

"If it's going to help, I'll just go home."

"No, you mustn't. Sit down, Jen. Here, you have some breakfast, too.

152

"Jennifer, it may sound crazy. Right now Margo is hurt and jealous. But I've got an idea that if you were to stay, you could help tremendously."

"Lois, you can't mean that. I'm making her miserable."

"If Gary wanted her, he'd go after her. She has to learn that lesson. What I meant was, if she could see herself as an individual, instead of some kind of delicate, little, frail thing that someone has to take care of, it would be exactly what she needs. I think you can help her in a way I can't."

"The opposite seems to be happening. If she only wanted to do something on her own."

The telephone rang once, then twice. Unfortunately, Margo answered it with a sweet breathless hello, but on hearing it was Gary with only a hearty, hi-there-may-I-please-talk-with-Jennifer, Margo let the receiver drop. It must have been an effort for her to say in low, resentful tones. "For Jennifer."

"Hi, Jen, Gary here. There's a great French movie in San Francisco tonight. I wonder if you've seen it."

"I've never seen a French movie at all."

"Great. Shall we go?"

"Well, yes, but . . ." Her voice dropped to a whisper that she hoped would be inaudible to everyone. "But Gary, couldn't Margo come with us? Make it a double date."

"Why not? I'd been hoping to be with you alone, but we can all go. What about Alan? He's really crazy about Margo."

"They went to some movies last night, but

maybe they'd like to go again. Could you ask him?"

Margo had disappeared. Jennifer waited for the returning call and when Alan said it was a stroke of genius to have thought of it, Jennifer's conscience rested more easily. Now Margo would have a chance to get Gary back if she wanted him or if he wanted her. What a strange way to think about people, as if it were some kind of taffy-pulling contest.

Margo, sitting by the pool, was painting her.

"There's my cousin, all smily and cheerful," Margo said venomously. Jennifer paid no attention.

"Margo, would you like to double-date tonight with Gary and Alan? We're going to San Francisco to see a French movie."

"Whose idea is this?" Margo asked guardedly, less angry now.

"Mine. I thought I'd like to have you with us. It might change things. I know you like being with Gary." There, she could not offer more, but Margo remained silent and went back to painting her nails. At last she turned to Jen.

"I don't know what your little game is, but okay, I'll go. There's nothing else to do."

"Margo, there's so much . . ."

But there was no talking with her. She got up, dove into the pool, disappeared from view for a moment, and then swam the length of the pool, probably ruining the job she had just done on her toenails. She kicked up a constant splash of white water to drown out Jen's words.

154

18.

Margo owned all the latest records and these she played as loudly as she could, as if to throw a wall of sound around her. Even so, the telephone pierced through the wailing of the latest rock star she "adored," and she dashed from her room to pick up the phone. A breathless hello, and then she dropped the receiver.

"For you, of course," she said, standing by the phone and making no pretense of giving Jennifer any privacy. "You get all the calls."

"No, I don't, silly," Jennifer said. Gary had left town suddenly and although it puzzled Jennifer, it actually upset Margo, making her more touchy than usual.

"Hello, Jennifer. Remember me? Barbara Blaine. I met you at Cindi's last week. I wondered if you'd like to come over for lunch and a swim."

"Thanks, I'd love to come," Jennifer said, catching Margo's unwavering eye, "only I'd planned to be with my cousin, Margo, today."

"Well, wouldn't she like to come, too?"

"I'll ask her."

Margo's resentment changed to surprise

and she nodded her head with more eagerness than she had shown in some time. Barbara explained how to get to her house on the outskirits of town, and Jennifer promised to be there.

"Hey — Barbara Blaine! Nice going. It was nice of you to ask me, too," Margo said with grudging thanks. "Barbie's in LaClique, but kind of distant, too. I mean, she never invites anyone to her house. Her mom's really prominent."

"I should say so," Lois said as she overheard the conversation. "She's a lawyer and she has her finger in a million San Francisco pies. Well, Jennifer, you're plunging right into the social swim, aren't you?"

"Am I? All I know is that I'm having the most terrific time ever, thanks to both of you."

At last everything was coming together and Gary had been the catalyst, for she had hardly been noticed before he began paying attention to her. Now there wasn't time enough for everything that could be done. In the morning, tennis with Gary, very often rides on the Suzuki, long thrilling rides; tamer bicycle rides with Cindi or Marcia, but pleasant enough; occasional treats to the theater in San Francisco by Lois; afternoons beside swimming pools; and evenings with Gary, sometimes alone, sometimes in the company of others. The double-dating with Margo and Alan had not worked out well after all, as Margo had foolishly insisted on clinging to Gary, which irritated him although he loved the flattery of it. However, when six or eight members of LaClique decided to do something together, Margo and Alan were always included along with Jennifer and Gary.

Jennifer wrote to her family frequently, telling Terry about the thrill of going to live plays and describing her progress in tennis and some of the lovely homes she visited. But she was careful not to talk of Gary as anything but one of Margo's friends.

"I'm having the most exciting summer ever!" she wrote. "There's nothing to do here but have a great time."

The Blaine house was perhaps more luxurious than the others, and the swimming pool considerably larger, but the party hardly differed from others Jennifer had attended. Half a dozen girls jumped or dived neatly into the pool, swam, sunned themselves lazily, and listened to records, sometimes singing along with them. Luncheon was an enormous glass bowl of fruit salad and iced tea.

She found no difficulty in making superficial friendships and since she felt herself only a visitor, said little.

"Hey, Jennie, what are you dreaming about? Gary, I'll bet," a girl Jennifer hardly knew teased.

"Actually, I'm not dreaming about him or anyone," she said, smiling guiltily.

"You may as well confess it. Everyone dreams about Gary."

"He's teaching you tennis, isn't he? You really score."

"He just thinks everyone should know how to play. I'm only a beginner," Jennifer said.

"You better watch out. There's a lot of games he's going to want to teach you," someone said in an emphatic way and a murmur of agreement followed. Possibly Gary was simply using her, testing her, as apparently he had done with others.

Talk shifted to chatter about boys they had met outside LaClique, a discussion of the problems other members had, about college coming up, about the weekends when they would go to meet their fathers.

"It's such a drag," Carol sighed. "So forced."

"I like being able to get away, but my mother gets so stewed up about it each time, it takes a week to get over it."

She had heard this talk many times before, as if parents were problems their children had to solve, rather than the other way around. She found a sadness in this. They were for the most part very pretty girls, intelligent enough, possibly lazy as they stretched out around the patio sunning themselves, smoking, rubbing oil over their skin, and letting the afternoon drift away.

"Have you received your invitation to the biggie? Diane Burton's end-of-summer thing?"

"She hasn't sent them out yet. We'll probably be invited."

"It's always such a great bash."

158

"But I think it's stupid; not the dance, that's terrific. But dressing formally. We just don't do that around here."

"It's a drag, but the Burtons come from the East and think we're deprived because we go around in jeans. So it's formal dress. What are you going to wear?"

Jennifer paid little attention to the conversation that followed; who would be invited, what they would wear, and so on, but when someone casually mentioned the date, August 30th, she pricked her ears.

August 30th. On the 31st judging would begin at the State Fair. And she wouldn't be there! Most likely she wouldn't be invited to the big dance the girls were talking about, since she hardly knew Diane Burton, but she wouldn't be at the Fair either. She gazed into the gleaming blue waters of the pool and remembered the last two years at the Fair, about the excitement of getting up early, loading the sheep into the truck, and driving to Sacramento. She could see herself in the stalls, calming the excited animals she would exhibit, cleaning them, currying them, and the conversation that followed: who would be invited, what they would wear, and so on, but talking with the visitors passing through. She would spend several nights at the dormitories, meeting exhibitors from all over the state, eating with them, strolling through the Midway at night with them. She thought once more about the mounting excitement as she would lead her sheep to the pavilion where they would be judged and holding them as the judges walked around them, writing in their books. How her heart would beat when the awards were made! It was as if all the work she had done during the year was climaxed in that moment.

And this year she wouldn't be there.

If she thought of it much more, she would be in danger of crying.

"Hey, I'm going in!" she announced with surprising energy, and so got up, performed a fairly handsome dive, and swam as fast as she could up and down, up and down, up and back again.

"Wasn't it great? Didn't you love their house? You were sure quiet, but I had a wonderful time," Margo said as they returned home late that afternoon.

"I want to talk with you for a minute, Jennifer. About Gary."

Would it be dreadful, more accusations?

"I wasn't going to do this, but since you saw that I was invited to Barbie's, I'll tell you. You're a little worried about Gary, aren't you? Going down to Big Sur or Carmel for several days and not telling you what he is going to do there. Just disappearing. And last week when he took off for Berkeley all of a sudden. It bothers you, doesn't it?"

"If he doesn't want to tell me about it, it's his right. I don't own him," Jennifer said, althought these absences puzzled her.

"This is how he is, Jennifer. The way he does things. He wants people to follow him and adore him, but he won't let himself be easily had. If you know what I mean. He wants to be the one leading and this is one way he does it. He's done this to other people, too."

"Oh, has he?" Jennifer asked, determined to appear indifferent, but it was one more thing that weighed on her mind. She would not cling, would not beg or demand to know where he had been. And yet he had confided he was afraid that he was falling in love with her. Never had he met anyone like her. She was changing, growing, and it thrilled him.

"Okay, you don't want to talk about it. But one thing about LaClique. We cue each other."

"Thanks for telling me," Jennifer said in a low voice, putting down her Coke. It was then that she noticed a letter waiting for her.

"A letter from Terry!" she cried, as if nothing could have delighted her more. She tore it open.

Dear Jennifer:

I'm bushed, but Mom says I should write to you because I owe you two letters.

Next week I'm going to 4-H camp.

We finished doing the apricots and now we're in the middle of peaches. You know what it's like. We've been canning, freezing, making pies, and jams. All that. This year Bruce helped us out and it was fun, some of the time, but we all missed you. Russ drops in almost every day to check on your sheep and to help

Bruce. He says he'll make a first rate rancher. Russ always make a GREAT POINT of asking if we've heard from you, but he asks in a quiet way as if he'd just thought of it. Ha ha ha! It doesn't fool anyone.

I sure hope Lois invites me to come and stay with her. Wow, would I love it. Have a great time. When are you coming home?
WRITE
Love and kisses,
Terry.

Jennifer, moved by her sister's letter in a most unexpected way, felt the pangs of having missed something. Only last summer in the heat of the kitchen, she had wished she could skip it all and lie in a hammock to read and sip lemonade all afternoon.

Now she thought of what it was like to be there during the hot days in late July when the peaches came on. Her brother bringing lug after lug to the back hall, she and Terry and her mother selecting the large, handsome peaches, each one perfect, slipping off the fuzzy rosy skins, slicing the fruit in huge stainless steel bowls for freezing. Her mother wiping her forehead and wondering if this year she would do well to experiment with a ginger peach preserve. Somehow the hot days slipped by quickly. They would have giggled a lot. In the late afternoon Russ might bicycle over with a jar of whipping cream as a present, and he might ask Jennifer to go swimming, or Mrs. Cowles would urge him to stay for dinner. He would admire the rows of jars filled with peaches as they cooled on the counter, and the dozen pies waiting to be wrapped and frozen, and the peach cobbler that would make dessert for that night's dinner.

It all seemed so far away.

Margo had disappeared into her room, shutting the door behind her, and nobody knew where Lois was. Jennifer would gladly have made dinner, but in the past when she had offered to do so Margo had said anything she made would be too fattening and Lois had explained, "We don't bother with cooking, dear. It's so easy to use the frozen dinners."

Jennifer looked out of the window, caught a view of an empty golf course, behind which the hills with their eucalyptus trees and clinging houses glowed in the light of the setting sun. It was beautiful, wasn't it? Then why did she feel a certain yawning emptiness? And why could she not stop thinking of home?

19.

For the next three days Jennifer devoted herself to cheering up Margo, not an easy task, but taking a ride to the beach one day, going to movies at night, and helping Margo with her math before the final exam brought about a closeness, almost as if they were sisters.

And then Gary called. Margo shrank into her room while Jennifer answered, surprised at the way her heart leaped at the sound of his voice.

"Hello, hello! Jen? How I've missed you. Did you forget everything you've ever learned about tennis?"

"No, teacher. I hope not. Shall we try it and see?"

"Tomorrow morning. But I can't wait until then to see you. How about dinner tonight at this little Italian restaurant I happen to know about."

"I can't resist!" she had laughed as he told her he would call for her at six-thirty.

Margo would sulk. No doubt she would repeat her old refrain, "If it weren't for you

164

butting in, Gary and I would be together. We were just like that before you came."

Jennifer had explained. "I don't *own* Gary. He's free to do anything he likes. I'm sorry, Margo, but that's how it is."

The hurt expression on Margo's face had shamed her. Nevertheless she would see Gary that evening. She stretched out lazily, bathed, read one of the romances Lois had let her take and found it silly. And yet she had never felt more romantic than now, as she waited for Gary.

"How did you ever find this place? It's just tucked away,"

"Aha! The shadow knows!" Gary quipped. A waiter led them to a table in the corner, where the light was not too bright, a candle in a green glass candlestick, a single rose in a vase, the usual red-checkered table cloth.

"This place isn't all that secret. And now tell me, how is everything going, Jen? As glowing as you look?"

"Am I glowing? I can't imagine why," she said, pretending to flirt.

"It's all that milk you drink," he teased, touching her cheek to show he was joking. "How about a touch of red vino with our lasagna tonight?"

"Why not?"

Jennifer was on the verge of asking him where he had been and what he had done, but remembered Margo's advice about Gary's tactics. She would play it cool then. She asked simply, "Did you have a good time?"

165

His eyes danced. "A lovely time, thank you."

He offered no explanation and if he had expected her to fret or become unduly inquisitive, he must have been disappointed. "How's your summer?"

"Going too fast, Gary. I wish it could stay summer forever." Now that she was with Gary, she meant it. The bouts of homesickness seemed hardly serious.

"It won't last forever, but hang in there. There's still time. You're beginning to open up now. When you first came you were like a tightly closed flower. Now you're unfurling."

"Very poetic."

He tasted the wine the waiter had brought, judged it all right, and poured Jennifer's glass. She enjoyed his attentions, his ease with words, his natural poise. If only Russ were as facile, how perfect he would be. If he were to take her to some such restaurant as this, although there were no restaurants at all for miles and miles near Grant, he would never think to tell her she "glowed."

"Before I forget, I have something to ask you. Or to tell you, Jennifer," he said with the utmost seriousness. "At first I wasn't sure that I would ask you this, but now I'd say you are learning to *go for it*, aren't you?"

"I don't know what you mean."

"It means . . ." he paused thoughtfully, tried the lasagna, pronounced it perfect, and then continued. "It's a lifestyle, a way of viewing everything. It means you pursue your own happiness because nobody else is going

166

to do it for you. You catch the golden moment; you don't wait and wait for something to happen. You don't postpone life."

Her face was serious as she studied his, for although he smiled, he meant what he said. Then she burst into a laugh that was a gesture of frustration. "I don't really know what you're talking about."

"All right. When you live on the ranch you have duties; you get up, milk the cow, do whatever you do to your lambs and chickens, etc. . . . Everything is set out for you; no surprises. You can't take a holiday without it hurting pretty much. Here, you see your whole life as a holiday. Why not?"

"Well, it's not really like that either. If I didn't want to have lambs, I wouldn't. But in a way, you're right. Holidays aren't easy to come by. But then, there are other things. I know what *you* mean. You like being spontaneous. Sort of 'right there,' if you know what *I* mean."

"You're learning. I'd like to be your teacher. In tennis. In other ways, too. I think I could make you happy."

"Is that what you wanted to ask me?"

"Actually, I want to take you to the August Hop. Don't tell me Margo hasn't been talking about that."

"You mean that dance the Burtons give every year? I've heard of it."

"Let's you and I go together."

"But I haven't been invited. I was once introduced to Diane. We said hello. End of acquaintance."

"Silly Jennifer! I've received my invitation and I can take anyone I please."

"Thank you, Gary. I'd really love to go. I heard it was really the big splash of the summer, but some of the girls were objecting about having to go formal."

"Don't let them fool you. They may wear jeans everywhere, but secretly they love getting dressed up. And I'd love to see you in an evening gown."

She laughed, glad now that she had brought her formal pink dress.

"And then, I hope you know about the three-day party that follows. No? Well, Mark Holmes' parents have a beach house on the coast and every year, following the Hop, perhaps ten of us, sometimes more, sometimes less, go there for three great days."

"Fantastic! What do you do there?"

"Whatever we feel like doing. We play. Go fishing, crabbing, snorkeling, diving. Too bad we can't go water skiing but the salt water is hard on skiis. If Joe McFee comes up this year, we'll have some hot music going the whole time. Barbecues on the beach. Lots of beer. We all have wheels in case we want to go somewhere."

Jennifer smiled but hesitated. Gary caught the note of uncertainty and took her hands in his.

"Jennifer, this will be an initiation for you. The real thing. I don't mean the stupid, silly things people do in fraternities and sororities; nothing like that. I'm talking about an initiation into a new way of living. I want you to

168

really experience what it is to be free and to learn what it is you want to do. There's something else I want to do, too, with you. I know somebody who has horses there. We can go riding along the beach together at dawn. The horse you'll ride is all white; I've had her before. I'll ride a black roan. We'll experience this together."

"It sounds like a dream."

"It is. You and I will get to know each other very well. I want to introduce you to the wonderful sense of being your own self. The joy of being."

"Exciting!" she giggled nervously. Gary had never looked more appealing, nor had he ever spoken with more conviction. He was offering her what she wanted . . . the lightness of being freed from every duty but one, the sense of being alive. Water, sun, air, a beach, friends . . . here was the T.V. drama coming to life. So why did she hesitate?

"You don't really need time to think it over, do you?"

"Thanks for asking. I'd love to come."

20.

School was over for Margo. With Jennifer's last-minute help, she had barely managed to pass the exam. And now, as Jennifer came in after a demanding game of tennis with Gary, Margo announced with marked coldness, "I'm going shopping with Marcia and Cindi to find something to wear to the August Hop. Just the three of us."

"I hope you find something nice," Jennifer said, aware that she had been purposefully left out. Well then, she would stay home and work on the white sweater she was crocheting.

As Margo left the kitchen, Lois apologized. "I'm sorry, Jennifer. You know very well if she didn't have her mind on Gary all the time, she'd be your best friend. I had so hoped that would happen."

"I did, too, Lois. Margo is so special. Why do things have to happen this way? It *would* be Gary who likes me and I feel awful that this hurts Margo; it's all so mixed up."

It was another gray day outside. Most of the mornings here seemed to be enshrouded in cool, gray fog. At first it had seemed a romantic, pearly gray, and when the sun chose to come out at three or four in the afternoon, it became a glorious spectacle.

170

On this gray, colorless morning, Jennifer knew that at home the hot, smiling, summer sun would be shining openly and brilliantly and somehow life would be simpler, without all the personal complications and conflicts that seemed to fill her cousin's house. She should go home; and yet she stayed as if there were something as yet unfinished. Nor could she bear the thought of not going to the August Hop and the beach party afterward.

Lois lit a cigarette, sipped her morning cup, and sighed, not bothering to hide her sadness. "Jennifer, love, I'm tired of staying home. Ted is away. Let's go out. I can't remember. Have you ever seen Sausalito?"

"No, I don't think so."

"Good. We'll go there. I want to find a present for your mother's birthday and we can have lunch. It's the most charming place."

Once more Lois became the vivacious aunt who had visited the Cowles' ranch. After they both showered and dressed, they rode in the Triumph along the highway, turning off at Sausalito, the town that perched on the waters of San Francisco Bay. Here the morning sparkled and Jennifer was enchanted with the house boats, the narrow streets with their older houses that perched perilously on a steep hill, and the tiny shops everywhere. Jennifer wondered why Margo had never suggested going there, but did not fret about it, since Lois turned out to be more delightful than ever. She must show Jennifer this shop, and then that darling place, and

171

still another place where the sweaters fairly took Jennifer's breath away. She also chose a present for her mother's birthday, a brass jewel box in the shape of a heart. Lois commended her on her good taste. The day was flying fast and soon Lois cried she was famished and Jennifer must be starving.

They sat on painted, white, garden chairs on a deck that stretched from the restaurant to the water's edge. A waiter brought iced coffees and green leafy salads.

"Sometimes it's easier to talk when you're away from home, isn't it?"

"I think so. Russell and I always go off by ourselves when we want to discuss something serious."

"Oh, Jennie, I love being with you, love having you with us."

"And I adore you, Lois. I really do." Jennifer had never been more sincere, but did not know how to say she felt the sadness in her aunt's life. At the moment they were understanding each other very well.

"Do you miss your charming friend, Russell?"

"Of course. We're good friends."

"Only friends? Is he in love with you?"

"I don't know, Lois. He never talks about it. Maybe."

"Men! Who ever knows what goes through their minds. They are such puzzles. It's best to be wholly independent. Then you can take care of yourself. If I could only teach that to Margo, but she's so confused. Does she seem confused to you?"

"She seems lost. As if she has no direction."

"Exactly. Poor mouse, her life has had its complications. Her father took his own life; did she ever tell you that? She's lived here and there, always with men who pretended to be her father, but it never quite works out. I'm still hoping that with Ted, it might. Of course, some youngsters turn out magnificently after stormy childhoods."

"And some dive bomb, even though their environment seems ideal. I've seen that happen in Grant and in Freeville, at school."

"You seem so sensible, Jennifer. I hope you're sensible about Gary."

"He's very kind. He never pressures me. Why do you keep warning me about him?"

Lois lit a cigarette, blew away smoke over the blue waters of the Bay. "He's clever. He's biding his time. You attract him because you're a hard one to push over, but he's broken many hearts, like Margo's. I never know whether to wipe her eyes and hold a handkerchief to her nose or whether I should simply spank her."

Jennifer laughed. "It's not easy, is it? I wish I could help her."

"I think you can, if the opportunity comes up. She does like you, you know. And you've already done something. She's never been invited around as much as she has since you've been here. You've made quite a splash."

"Me? I can't believe it."

"Listen, Jennifer, I'm very serious now. I want to invite you to live with us this year, transfer to school here. Ted and I have talked

173

about it. We both think a great deal of you. He said he liked the idea of 'two daughters.' But I'm thinking about you, too, Jennifer."

"This is all too much," Jennifer said. A waitress brought her a bowl of lemon sherbet, but she could hardly touch it.

"Ranch life is hard. You know that your mother is forever working. Do you really want to do this with your life? Or would you rather stretch your wings and get into a more exciting life? Maybe a different career."

Jennifer averted her eyes. Pictures of Gary kept flashing through her head. He would be in his apartment in San Francisco and would want her to visit him. He had promised they would go mountain climbing, water skiing, and of course tennis always. She would learn his philosophy: go for it! It was clear here was her chance, now or never.

"Don't frown, Jennifer. You'll want to think about it. You don't have to decide this minute. And of course we'll have to talk with your father and mother. And now, aren't you going to try that sherbet? May I have a taste of it?"

"It's so exciting and so scary to think of staying on I don't know what to think, but I appreciate your asking me," Jennifer said, determined to smile now and put off the difficult decision as long as she could.

The next day a letter came from Russell. It had been a wet day, dripping with fog, and the tennis lesson had been postponed. Mists blotted out the landscapes and Jennifer had

174

to put on a sweater to keep warm. She pulled the letter out from its envelope slowly in order to savor it.

Dear Jennifer,
Sometimes I almost feel sorry for you, missing the summer here. The weather is practically perfect, hot but good. We've completed the haying now.

Yesterday Bruce told me about some far-out plans of his to raise squab. At first it seemed far-fetched, but I've looked into it, and what do you know, there are good markets for it in Sacramento. Bright young brother!

I'm beginning to make decisions about which animals I'll be showing at the Fair. All to be Grand Champions of course! Wish you were here. You always have good sense in these matters, although my decisions have just about been made.

Don't forget. Your applications are on file at the Fair.

The moon was full last night, so I took a long, lonesome ride on a new quarterhorse my mother has just purchased. Flash may be a little difficult to control, but he'll be fine. The moonlight has never been more brilliant, shining over the fields and hills and orchards, so damn beautiful. I think you would have liked it.

                              Yours,
                              Russell

A longing to see Russ came upon Jennifer with such intensity that she had to check the sudden urge to telephone him. To have missed even one moonlight ride now seemed unforgivable, yet it had been her choice to leave for the summer.

She read the letter again. He had not mentioned being with any other girl. Good! But he had not stated an overwhelming love for her, either, signing the letter with a formal "yours" instead of "love."

I must go home, she thought one minute, and in the next she wondered how she could possibly do so. She would miss Gary so much.

21.

Where had the time gone? Here it was five days before the August Hop and Jennifer had not quite made up her mind about the party after the Hop, or whether she would accept her aunt's invitation to stay for a year. No matter how she thought of it, weighing pros and cons, it invariably ended in a perfect draw.

The game with Gary had gone particularly well early that morning. She had come home to make breakfast and then bicycled downtown to the Knittery to pick up some more yarn that she would need for the sweater. She was letting herself back into the condominium when she heard raised voices from the kitchen. Lois and Margo arguing. Margo's voice growing higher and more petulant, while Lois', low and increasingly determined, was showing a strength Jennifer had not expected.

"You're going too far, Margo. You will not buy it and charge it. You'll have to find something else."

"But this dress is all *me*. I have to look marvelous at the Hop, it's essential. It's the most important evening in my whole life."

177

"My darling girl, no *one* evening will ever be the most important evening in your life. All right, I can't expect you to see that. But in plain language, we cannot afford two hundred dollars for a dress you will wear once, or even twice, or even fifty times."

"But *you* have a closet full of clothes. Cindi and Marcia bought their dresses at Madame Irina's the very first day, without even thinking about the price."

"That's their business, not ours. Now listen, Margo, and try to get some sense into that head of yours. Ted is extremely generous and we're not going to take any undue advantage of him. I'm going to have to cut way back, too. Times are not that easy."

"Oh, no! Does that mean you and Ted are going to split?"

"Certainly not. But it's time you became a little sensible. You don't have to go to the most expensive boutique in town."

"Then I won't go to the August Hop. I simply won't go."

"All right, don't go."

"And its all *her* fault!" Margo cried. "Why did you ever ask her here?"

The slamming of a bedroom door finished the conversation.

Margo should have been an actress, she weeps so tragically, Jennifer thought as she took up her sweater once more. She had also bought some mohair that would make a sweater for Terry's Christmas present, and she was thinking how comforting it was to work with her hands, but not with Margo in such obvious misery. Half an hour later Jennifer knocked on the door softly.

"Margo? It's me. May I talk with you."

"No. Go away."

"Please, Margo. I have something to tell you about that dress you want. Something important."

Margo, red-eyed, thin, more an undernourished waif than elfin beauty, opened the door no more than five inches and peered out.

"What about that dress?" she asked sullenly.

"I'd like to see it on you."

"What's the use? They won't let me get it. I think my mother even called Madame Irina.

"You have terrific taste and I'd like to see you in that dress, even if you can't buy it."

"Oh, you're going to lend me the money I suppose?"

"I would if I could. Really."

This last stopped Margo, for she couldn't argue with it. "I don't know why you want to see it, Jen. But I'm bored staying here."

"All right. So let's go."

Margo, unconvinced, nevertheless pulled on jeans, slipped into a T shirt, and brushed her black hair.

Madame Irina's was a boutique that was clearly a few levels above the teen-oriented shops Margo usually visited. Soft, coral carpets, a sophisticated quietness in the decor, and a guitar playing soft jazz. Madame Irina, black hair pulled back in a coil and eyes

179

sporting half-inch lashes, barely repressed a sigh as she saw the girls.

"May I please try this on?" Margo asked with a certain unctuous sweetness as she took a dress from the rack. Jennifer had the impression of soft materials laid in tones of lavender and violet. "I'd like to show it to my cousin."

Madame Irina's lips hardened, but she gave in. "Unless you buy it, this will be the last time. All right?"

Margo disappeared into the tiny dressing room and emerged a few minutes later, still pale and red-eyed, but lovely, certain that this dress was meant for her alone.

"You're right, Margo. It's a dream," Jennifer said, studying it carefully while she tried to appear the casual companion. Chiffon squares were tipped on the bias so they hung from the waist, producing a hem that dipped with alluring unevenness. A dancer could have worn such a dress, turning so that the material would billow out and follow her movements. One shoulder was bared while the other let a rosy length of diaphanous violet drift from a velvet ribbon at its apex.

"It's your dress, no doubt about it," Madame Irina agreed.

"Let me help you," Jennifer said crowding into the dressing room with Margo. There she examined the dress carefully, inside and out.

"And so now what? Satisfied?" Margo asked as she put her jeans and shirt on again. Jennifer put her finger over her mouth. Shh!

They thanked Madame Irina so profusely,

180

she could not possibly have chided them and left the shop. Once they were outside, Jennifer said. "Margo I can make that dress for you if we can find the material. At least I can come very close. There's actually a pattern something like it."

"I suppose you learned all this in 4-H."

"As a matter of fact, I did. Listen here, Margo." Jennifer was coming close to losing her temper. "I've taken a lot from you ever since I've been here and now I'm offering to help you out. I'll even treat you to the material and pattern, which won't be cheap. But I want you to know I've been modeling clothes I made in 4-H at the big finals contest ever since I've been twelve years old. And I've won prizes, too. Some of those 4-H girls are practically professional in their work and if you want to keep putting it down, we can just forget the whole thing."

"I'm sorry. I'm not used to having people do things for me. Do you really think you could make a dress like that?"

"Of course. At least it would come close. Shall we find a pattern?"

Now it was Margo who rushed toward *Fabulous Fabrics*, while Jennifer begged her to remember whether Lois had a sewing machine or not. She thought there might be one in the back of a closet. They spent the next hour and a half poring over the pattern books, finally chosing one that pleased Margo. They chose the materials carefully and Jennifer insisted on laying out the pattern pieces so she wouldn't buy more of the expensive material than she would actually need. Thread, bindings, ribbons, a touch of velvet . . . and Margo blurted her embarrassment when Jennifer insisted it would be her gift.

They bicycled home quickly and spent the day ironing the pattern carefully and fitting it to the fabric. Margo could baste and hem, but knew little else. Jennifer explained everything as she went along and Margo's eyes brightened as she took it all in. They barely stopped for lunch, this time Jennifer insisting that Margo share an omelet with her and a slice of toast as well. Margo placed a stack of records on her stereo, toning it down, and together the girls worked, Margo meekly doing everything that Jennifer told her.

"I love this. Why didn't I ever do it before?"

"It's not too late. I think you have a good touch."

"Maybe I'll become a designer."

"Why not?" Jennifer said. Her cousin was a dreamer, but this was perhaps the first positive statement she had made. Jennifer said nothing about the grueling training a good designer must undergo. Margo would find out for herself soon enough.

The afternoon flew. They heard Lois sigh as she came in and then she stopped short. "What's this?" she cried.

Jennifer was sitting at the sewing machine and Margo, sitting on a kitchen stool, was hemming the underskirt, which the transparent chiffon required. Strips of pale chiffon were scattered over the living room floor, a length of violet chiffon hung over the

182

abstract sculpture, and the pattern pieces that had not yet been ready to be put away seemed to stand lightly on their tissue folds.

"You're *sewing*? You found my machine?"

"Don't look so astonished, Mom. You've seen people sew before."

"But not you, darling. And Jennifer, what are you making?"

"Look!" Margo grabbed the pieces of chiffon, held them to her, and turned slowly around as if she were already dancing.

Lois flopped into one of the chairs. "It's too much for me. But I'll tell you right now. It's a true surprise. Wait till I tell Ted!"

Lois had to drive them to bed that night or they would have sewed until dawn. Even so, Margo crept into Jen's room and sat at the foot of her bed, a different Margo, straightforward and rational.

"Jen, have you decided to stay with us for the year?"

"Honest, I just don't know. Usually I'm decisive. Maybe after the dance or the beach party I'll see it more clearly."

Margo interrupted. "Jennie, there are some things you ought to know. About LaClique. About the beach party. Tell me, what do you think of the kids you've met?"

"I like them, I think, some more than others. They're different. But it bothers me when they drink and smoke too much. My personal prejudice. Anyway, I don't judge people."

"Maybe you ought to. So far we're pretty

tame compared to some groups around here. But when we get alone at the beach and there aren't any chaperons, it can get wild. It's not like a 4-H girls' pajama party."

"So I understand."

"The main idea is to have a good time and if someone doesn't join in, they aren't always very polite about it."

"It's obvious I'm an outsider, but if I'm with Gary and everyone likes him, does it really matter if I keep to my own standards? I'd never dream of imposing them on anyone else."

Margo shook her head and talked slowly as if she had to explain to a child what it was all about. "Don't you know what Gary wants, what he's leading up to? You can't be that naive. Of course, if you want to go along with him, that's your business."

"Margo, I know very well what I'm willing to do and what I'm not going to do. I have a mind of my own."

Margo smiled slowly. "I know. That's why you might have a hard time with LaClique. And with Gary. Think about it. Anyway, I don't want you to get hurt, whatever you decide to do. You've been terrific to me. Making the dress and all. I'll never forget it as long as I live. And this is something I've never said to anyone, Jennifer, in all my life."

"Thanks, Margo." Her hand reached out over the coverlet and clasped her cousin's. Then they said good night and Margo tiptoed back to her room.

22.

"Maybe you'd like to read this letter from your mother, Jennifer," Lois said, handing her the stationery with Emily Cowles' even handwriting

> Dear Lois:
> It's easier for me to write than to telephone. It's generous of you and Ted to offer to let Jennifer stay with you during her senior year, although I confess the idea shocks us. Of course, we've missed Jennifer all this summer, but we mustn't think of ourselves. We want the best for all our children, but it's not easy to know what's best. Perhaps Jennifer would do well to think this through carefully and judge for herself. We'll be waiting to hear from her or from you.
>
> Love,
> Emily

"Oh, Lois, that makes it harder than ever to decide."

Nor did it help that the letter came on the morning of August 30th, while Jennifer was slowly packing the bag with the clothes she would need for the three-day party at the beach. Gary had explained the plans that had developed. He and Alan would call for her and Margo; the dance would last until three or four in the morning, at which point they would all go out for breakfast and then head directly for the beach.

Margo, thoroughly delighted with her dress, was talking with Lois about studying design and fashion.

"I appreciate everything *you've* done, Jennie. You really are like a wonderful sister. But I can't forget it's Gary who's taking you to the dance." She spoke ruefully whenever she mentioned Gary as if she were a spoiled child. Jennifer's patience was close to ending.

"Well, if you say pretty please, maybe Gary will take you *home* from the dance. But it's not my problem."

Lois entered Jennifer's room and perched on the edge of the bed. "Seriously, Jennifer, you'd better make up your mind. There's one week before school begins here. I guess it begins at the same time in Freeville."

"I know, Lois. It's such a hard decision. I just can't think straight."

"Want to toss a coin?"

"I think I'll take a swim. Want to come?"

"Maybe later," Lois said uncertainly.

Jennifer found it a relief to dive into the pool in back of the Knolls and swim long laps up and down. Someone had left a transistor radio and the soft easy music eased the tenseness of the day. Jennifer swam twenty-five laps, and then climbed out of the pool, and stretched out on a beach towel while the sun shone down.

Life was so easy here. No chores, no work, no guilt for letting a day slip through her fingers as she was doing that day, as she had done all summer. She could be happy here. And if LaClique didn't want her, there were others who would welcome her friendship. Better classes would be offered in the school here then at Freeville High, she imagined. Weekends she would visit Gary in his San Francisco apartment or they would go water skiing, or up to the mountains to ski when it grew cold. She would take him home to visit the ranch. Here, there would always be something going on, movies, night clubs, rock concerts.

Gary was so special. So special. And he loved her. Perhaps it would be best to stay.

She drifted off to sleep, experiencing the painful intensity of dreams made in the light of the afternoon sun. In the dream she was at home. Her mother stood in a steaming kitchen, holding a pile of pies that reached to her chin. Outside the lambs were running this way and that, deeply disturbed. Her brother came running toward her with King, his handsome rooster, lying limp in his arms, the head hanging from its broken neck. She wanted to comfort him, but he couldn't see her. Then, with the jerky illogic of dreams, the family stood in the living room, all dressed soberly in their Sunday clothes, and presently the Steeles were there, too. She saw a funeral procession up a long hill. She cried out.

And then found herself sitting with Gary on the high rocks that overlooked the ocean, with the surf crashing beneath them, and he kept hissing, *This is what you want, isn't it? This is what you want,* as if ordering her to want it. She cried no, and then suddenly she was beside Russ at the State Fair and they were both dressed in their 4-H whites, leading long lines of steers and cows and lambs and horses to be judged, but there, too, she became invisible. She stood in front of Russ and shook him, but woke up before she knew whether he recognized her or not.

Her neck hurt where she had lain uncomfortably. She must have slept a long time. The dreams that had appeared so real she could have sworn they actually happened, left her exhausted.

"I'd give anything to be back there!"

She could see Russ as she had seen him on so many days before the Fair. He would be caring for the herd, carefully scrubbing and hosing down and grooming the champion animals he would show. She would be doing the same thing with her lambs. She would practice with them, leading them around the imaginary ring and pausing at attention while the judges examined each contestant. By this time she would have accustomed them to standing in correct stance. Her 4-H whites would be washed, ironed, and ready to wear. Her bags would be packed for the three nights she would stay at the Fair. And always, on the night before the Fair, no matter how busy they both would be, Russ would come to see her or she would visit him so they could share the mounting excitement of the big show together.

If only she were there . . .

She so wanted to see Russ. "Want" grew to "must," and so gathering up her towel, she flew up the stairs. Margo was off somewhere, and Ted, home for the weekend, sat with Lois in the living room while the giant T.V. blared out a report on some kind of game going on somewhere. At least it meant she could talk in private. She dialed the familiar number and to her surprise Russ answered on the first ring, almost as if he had been standing there, waiting. They used to joke about the ESP that seemed to exist between them. Now it seemed remarkable to Jennifer that this should be so.

"Hello, Russ? It's me, Jennifer."

"I could tell by the way the phone rang. How are you? Is everything all right?"

"Sure. Great. How are you doing?"

"All right. But I miss you, Jen."

For a second she dared not speak for her voice would betray her; then she recovered. "Big day tomorrow, right? Who are you taking to the Fair?"

"Reggie Three looks magnificent. Also Mavis Butterfield ought to do okay. Actually marvelously. A few calves. Mom will be taking Lady Ranelagh."

"It makes me so homesick to hear you talking about it. Russ, I wish I were there with all of you." Her voice broke and she wondered if he noticed.

"Hey, I thought you were having this glorious, fantastic time."

"Well, I am. In a way."

"I heard you were invited to take your senior year there instead of here. Are you going to do it?"

"Russ, I just can't decide. For the first time in my life I can't make up my mind. I know I'll have to. But anyway, there's this big dance tonight at the Tennis Club and a beach party afterward. I should know then."

"Jennifer, something's wrong."

"No, Russ, nothing's wrong. It's just that I was thinking about you and the Fair and sort of wishing I were there. Anyway, it's a little late for that. I want to wish you lots of good luck."

"Jennifer? Jennifer?" He wanted to get to her, but she couldn't hear him for the crowd at the T.V. game threw out a vast roar and then something must have happened at the other end of the wire, for she was cut off. It would not be the first time the rural telephone had failed.

She put back the receiver slowly and closed her eyes, wanting to retain the sound of Russ' voice as long as she could.

Lois knocked on the door of the bedroom where Jennifer lay on her bed, eyes wide open as she stared at a spot on the rug.

"Jen, darling, hadn't you better pack the things you're taking for the weekend, just in case we need to pick up something at the last minute?"

"I'll do it in a little while," Jennifer called.

"Jennifer, don't you feel well? You're so quiet today and tonight's the big night. Margo's so keyed up. Is anything wrong?"

"No, I'm fine, perfectly fine," Jennifer answered, lifting her head from the pillow and smiling falsely. Lois called out "all right" very softly and left, and Jennifer's smile faded. What was the matter with her? All summer long she had waited for this dance and now she feared it. The beach party was her chance to enact that fantasy she had entertained for so many months and yet it filled her with dread. Margo's warning echoed her own instinctive fears, that the party, without chaperons or restrictions of any sort, would become thoroughly wild. She would be expected to behave like the other guests, to drink, to smoke, to do whatever they did, and if she did not go along, she would not be tolerated.

But Gary would be there. He would protect her, she argued with herself. Against her will came the refrain of doubt. Would he allow her to do what she liked or would he twist logic so that she would do what he wished? Go for it! You have only one life so make the most of it! He could be so persuasive.

Everything was so mixed up. Here was a dream coming true and yet she would give anything if it weren't. Reluctantly, she got up and packed her bag for the weekend party.

23.

Time did strange things that day. It stood still. It dragged. It leaped ahead. Suddenly it was time to get ready. Both girls took long, bubbly baths. Jennifer was still in her robe as she helped Margo put on the new dress. She was truly happy with it as she paraded before her mother and Ted, turning slowly like a model, and then faster, like a dancer, so that the shimmery material flowed and fell gently in place when she stopped.

"Terrific," Ted said. For the first time he seemed truly pleased about Margo.

"Come on, I've got to finish this film. Have to get your picture," Jennifer cried.

"Please, stand here, against this window. Then we'll go out by the pool. And I want a shot of you on the steps."

They flew from one place to another, Jennifer excited about Margo and the way the dress had turned out, and more than that, the radiance that Jennifer had never before seen in her cousin.

"Jennifer, you've got to get dressed. I'll do your makeup if you like," Lois cried. Jennifer begged to take one more shot of Margo. Then she dressed quickly and sat with a towel around her neck while Lois expertly heightened her color and pulled her blonde hair to the top of her head, fastening it there with a comb on which were tied pink and white roses. Two curling, blonde strands fell, framing her face.

"Here, I'd like you to wear this," Lois said, offering Jennifer a crystal necklace. Jennifer drew in her breath at its beauty.

"It's real jewelry. Antique? I wouldn't dare."

Jennifer was tempted to take it, but in the end she chose to wear the tiny jade lamb on its gold chain. While Lois went to answer a phone call, Jennifer saw herself in the full-length mirror, flushing slightly with excitement. She knew that she had never looked better and found herself wishing almost immediately that Russ was there to see her.

The last time she had dressed like this, he had kept her waiting, but later he had urged her to drive the twenty miles it would take to get to the Prom, even if it meant making only the last dance. Now she was sorry she had refused. When she'd put the dress away the next morning, she had believed it was for the last time. Yet here she was wearing it.

Her skin had taken on a honeyed look during the summer, and her hair had lightened considerably in the sun. She had changed in other ways, too. Were there to be still further differences between the country cousin, Jennifer, and the girl reflected in the mirror?

Then the bell rang and a clamor of voices

and laughter filled the house. She recognized Alan's genial voice, Gary's charming patter, and Ted's bass words of welcome.

"Where are the girls?" she heard Gary ask.

"One more earring to go and I'll be there," she cried out, as she fastened the dangling crystal earrings that Lois had offered along with the necklace. These she could not refuse, loving the way they fragmented the light as she moved. She sprayed perfume over her skin and then appeared in the living room.

"Gary!" she cried. She had never seen him in evening clothes, the ruffled shirt, the polished black shoes, and his hair carefully trimmed. But he could hardly speak for true astonishment when Jennifer appeared. For once he found himself at a loss for words.

He walked up to her and kissed her.

"Isn't there supposed to be someone else?" Alan called out loudly.

Slowly, deliberately, Margo made her appearance. Alan's face burst into something like exhilaration. "What a vision! I can't believe it. Oh man, what be-aut-ti-ful girls!"

Chit-chat of sorts. And then it was time to leave. The canvas bags in which the girls had packed their clothes for the beach party would be put away in Alan's car. As in a dream, everyone was now saying good-bye, shaking hands with Ted, embracing Lois.

"I feel like the queen of something, but I'm not sure what," she cried and then became motherly. "Margo, Jennifer. Behave yourselves now. And don't drink."

"We'll bring 'em back safe and sound.

That's a promise," Gary said. Jennifer, seeing the worry in her aunt's eyes, embraced her, and at last the two couples left.

The road twisted up and down hills, passing through groves of eucalyptus and evergreens. Once Gary had stopped at a high spot from which the country spread below. "I'd like to hold on to this forever," Jennifer had said and he had answered gently.

"Nothing is forever, sweetie. It's all come and go. Haven't you learned that yet?"

The Tennis Club, a spacious, sprawling, redwood building on top of a hill, was intended to be impressive and Jennifer was duly impressed. The parking lot hidden behind a row of poplars was nearly full, and Alan hurried so that they wouldn't miss any more of the dancing. They could hear the music of a live band drifting through the gentle August night. Jennifer tried to imagine herself growing up here, maybe someday becoming a member of the Tennis Club, playing on the courts here, inviting friends to lunch. Gary stopped to embrace her.

"Jennifer, this is the beginning of the most beautiful weekend of our lives."

"That sounds like a line from a play, Gary."

"On my honor, I just made it up. It's true, you know. You and I will experience what we've never known before."

"Hey, we're supposed to be dancing. Come on!" Alan called.

The music had begun, soft, easy, lilting.

Later it would grow louder and wilder, but now a certain mellowness synchronized with the evening. How easy it was to dance with Gary! Jennifer tried to lose herself in the music. Gary's eyes never left her. An odd thought crossed her mind, that he was hypnotizing her.

The dance ended. And then Alan must dance with her and some other boys had come over. Jennifer noticed with satisfaction that several clustered around Margo and naturally she chose to dance with Gary, letting her pretty head rest on his shoulder for a brief moment. She was acting well, Jennifer thought, soft but not clinging.

Colored lights revolved. Several boys asked for the next dance, but Gary had come back. Everything was perfect. Why then did she feel so unable to enjoy it all?

"Are you all right?" he asked when the music stopped. "You looked so . . . mmmm . . . wistful, somehow."

"I'm having a wonderful time. It's a super dance," she lied, forcing a wide smile.

"Not so, Jennie. You can't fool Uncle Gary. Look, darling, this is one of the most beautiful dances you will ever find. Doesn't everyone look great? Romantic?"

"Truly. They ought to make a movie of it."

"I've been looking forward to this all summer, being here with the most exciting girl I've ever known. So why have the vibes changed?"

"You'll have to forgive me."

"Jennifer, come with me."

He led her outside to the patio. "Poor little bird. I can see there's a struggle going on. The cage is open. All you have to do is fly out, but you're afraid. Don't be, darling. I wouldn't let anyone or anything hurt you."

"Gary, I'm not exactly a little bird that's been locked up in a cage. It's just that I don't belong here. I made an awful mistake by staying so long."

"You sure picked a fine time to tell me. We're here. The party begins tomorrow."

"But, Gary, I didn't know. You're so great. You really are. I don't want to be difficult." She broke off suddenly. "We're at a dance. Let's dance, shall we? I hear something fast coming on."

"That's better. One thing about you. You always snap out of it."

Snap out of it, snap out of it! The words repeated themselves and she laughed falsely as if she were having the wonderful time she had expected to have.

Deliberately she faked smiles and made remarks she hoped were charming. She danced in a way that suggested she was happy, but finding it difficult to keep up the false small talk, told Gary she wanted to go to the Powder Room and would be right back. In the Powder Room one girl, who had apparently just been sick was helping another in the throes of losing her dinner. Their faces had turned a pasty white and strands of hair stuck to their cheeks. They looked as though they wanted nothing more than to lie down and sleep it off, but instead they spurred themselves on, washing out their mouths, repairing their makeup, and combing their hair before going back to the dance floor.

"If only I could learn to hold my liquor," one of them said.

Again Margo's words haunted Jennifer. Sane, sensible words. "It's not your kind of party, Jennifer. You don't know what you're getting into."

Reluctantly Jennifer went back to the dance floor. Gary suggested that a drink would do her good.

"No, thanks."

"Come on, Jennifer. I want you to be happy. You'll see how good it makes you feel. Come on."

"No, Gary. I don't want it. That's final," she said, surprised at her own strength. Surprising, too, was the expression of annoyance that she had never before seen on Gary's face. Would they fight then?

"Shall we dance?" she asked coyly. "I could *dance* forever."

"I'll bet you could," Gary said sardonically, "if it kept you from facing your problems."

He finished his drink with maddening slowness and then took her back on the floor. Some of his ugly mood vanished, but thoughts kept streaking through her head in a terrible confusion. This was Gary who had promised to open her life, to show her vistas she would not otherwise find. At the same time she knew she would not go to the beach party after all. But how could she get out of it?

"Get that frightened expression off your face," Gary ordered, and this time he was neither gentle nor smiling. "Anyone would think I was about to molest you right here on the dance floor."

"Don't be silly. Nobody would think that, least of all me," Jennifer answered, yet she no longer felt sure of anything. The lights flashed around the ballroom faster and faster as the music increased its tempo. Gary turned her around and around as if willing her to do what he wished, although she was getting dizzy and feared she would fall.

The music stopped in time. Before Gary could scold her, for he seemed about to do so, one of the attendants at the Tennis Club approached her.

"Pardon me, are you Jennifer Cowles?"

"Yes. Is something wrong?"

"I don't think so. There's someone here to see you. He seemed to think this was of utmost importance. If you'll come with me, please."

Jennifer, white-faced, asked Gary to pardon her as she followed the attendant down the length of the corridor to a small lounge. There, waiting for her, was Russ.

"Russ!"

Her voice rang with relief and joy. The attendant left the two of them alone as Jennifer rushed into his arms and without knowing why began to sob.

"Jen, hey, Jen? Aren't you glad to see me? What's all this with the tears?"

"I'm so glad to see you. I can't stop myself. Is everyone all right at home?"

"Sure. Of course."

Her sobbing turned to laughter, but the tears kept coming and then suddenly it was all over and she was herself again. "You'll never know how good it is to see you."

"Darling."

He had never called her that before.

"You never asked me why I came. If you'll stop bawling like a calf left out of the barn on a rainy night, I'll tell you. Maybe I'll tell you something else, too."

"Will you tell me the 'something' or the 'something else' first?" she asked.

"Later. Jen, it's so marvelous to see you. I just couldn't wait for you to make up your mind to come home. I had to come to get you."

"You look magnificent," she said, embarrassed, making small talk. "Must be your outfit." He grinned, for he was wearing what he always wore, jeans, boots, jacket, and the western hat lying on the sofa behind him.

Then, not knowing what struck her, she actually clung to him, sobbing with relief. "Russ, don't leave me here. Take me home. Will you, Russ, will you?"

"Sure. That's why I came. I knew something wasn't right. I just knew it. Besides, I couldn't see going to the Fair without you."

"I want to go there, too, with you, more than anything. Only I guess I won't have anything to show. I should've stayed home."

"Remember, I sent in your application?

Well, Terry, Bruce, and I have been scrubbing your not quite-so-clean little lambie pies for the occasion. We thought maybe you'd like to show Mork and Mindy."

"Will we get there in time?"

"If we leave now. I brought the pickup. We won't get lots of beauty sleep, but we can make it to the Fair."

Tears gone, she found herself laughing with relief. "How did you know where to find me?"

"I stopped at Lois'. She said she'd understand if you went back."

"I have to tell Gary and Margo."

"Yes, Jennifer, I think you have some explaining to do."

Jennifer turned around to see Gary standing there. Handsome as ever, but furious. Now she knew that underneath the smooth, calm sophistication, a fierce temper lay in wait. In a moment, she knew it was possible for him to become ugly. But she didn't have to fear him anymore, for Russ was there.

"Gary, this is my friend, Russell Steele. Gary Wilson. Gary has been kind to me. He's shown me Marin County and he's been teaching me tennis." None of this seemed to matter as the two men glared at each other.

Suddenly Margo appeared and said hello as Jennifer introduced her to Russ, but kept quiet in the growing tenseness of the situation.

"Gary, I'm sorry to say this. You've been terrific. I've liked being with you. You really have opened my eyes. But the truth is I don't belong here. I wasn't meant to 'go for it.' Please don't take it personally."

"And just how am I supposed to take a remark like that?"

"It's my fault. I should have thought out everything more clearly. But then you taught me I should do what I feel, that it's great to be spontaneous, and that I don't owe anything to anyone. So I'm going to follow your philosophy and do what I want. Which is, to go home. Russ came to get me."

"Was I ever wrong about you!" he said and stared at her coldly. "You'd rather go home and spend your life with a bunch of sheep and cows."

"Ranching has its own freedom," she said, "but if you've never experienced it, I couldn't expect you to know. Anyway, I think Margo would like to cheer you up, wouldn't you, Margo? She's better for you than I am, Gary. There, Margo, I said maybe Gary would take you home."

To her surprise, Margo shook her head. "I came with Alan and I'll stay with him. Sorry, but that's how it is. Jen, can I talk with you privately for just a minute?"

They moved out of hearing of the two men.

"Jennifer, I'll miss you so much. Now I really wish you were staying. We're just getting to know each other, aren't we?"

"Sure. I don't intend to be stuck in the country. And you can visit. Listen, I'm sorry about Gary, I think he really likes you."

"Only I'm not so sure that I really like him anymore. Jennifer, when he was talking to you and Russ he looked so ugly. Anyway, I really *do* like Alan. He's much nicer. Hey, will you and Russ come down to see us?"

"Thanks for asking. We'd love it. And you come to see us, too."

The girls hugged each other. Then Jennifer put her arms around Gary. She kissed him lightly on the cheek and then walked off with Russ into the cool, sweet August air.

As they drove back, Jennifer asked Russ to stop at the Lookout Point. "You can't see much now, but some weekend we'll want to come down. It's so very beautiful. And I want us to meet with my cousin and Alan, go on picnics, go to the coast together. Russ, it's glorious. And I want to see it with *you*."

"Is this the new lifestyle I keep hearing about?" he asked doubtfully.

"Not exactly. But I think we could use a little more style in *our* lifestyle, don't you? I'm glad I came here, Russ. It wasn't always easy, but I learned I don't fit here, because home is exactly right for me. I know it and I love it."

"I knew it would turn out like this, but at moments I got scared, Jennifer, afraid you'd find you liked this place better, that you'd find some handsome guy like that Gary."

"You're the handsomest guy I know," Jennifer said. "By the way, wasn't there something you were going to tell me?"

"Is now the time?" he asked and then, becoming serious, took her in his arms and kissed her as if he would never let her go.

"I've been thinking for a long time, Jennifer, that I love you so much it's all I can do to keep from telling you."

"Russ, why didn't you tell me this before?"

"I was afraid that I was just a friend. You never said anything about love."

Suddenly Jennifer began to laugh. "This is all so ridiculous. And now that that's clear, I'm so happy."

"Now that I think of it, maybe I am, too," Russell said.

Jennifer let her head rest on his shoulder as he drove east and north toward Grant. The first streaks of dawn lightened the sky as the truck drove up to the Cowles Ranch.

"Good timing!" Russell said. "We'll make it after all."